Splintered

Enjoy!

BP

Splintered

A New Orleans Tale

Brandi Perry

GOLD-BUG MYSTERIES
Columbia, South Carolina

Produced in the Republic Of South Carolina by

Gold-Bug Mysteries
An Imprint of

SHOTWELL PUBLISHING, LLC
Post Office Box 2592
Columbia, South Carolina 29202

www.ShotwellPublishing.com

Cover Photography & Design: Simms Brooks | www.SimmsBrooks.com

ISBN-13: 978-1947660090
ISBN-10: 1947660098

Chapter One

ROSS HANKINS FIDGETED with the skeleton key as he stood before the tall iron gate. It was February in New Orleans. The "Crescent City", which so tightly hugged the banks of the ancient Mississippi River, appeared unassuming and somewhat calm. Mere blocks from the French Quarter was this part of the city that never slept, the melting pot of the American South. It appeared tame, perhaps preparing itself for the upcoming Mardi Gras celebration. The silence boomed down the empty streets louder than any party on Bourbon Street could have, begging Ross to clench his trench coat a little tighter to his chest. The wind off the nearby Mississippi River barreled over Tchoupitoulas Street, through the narrow streets, and into the Garden District. His 6-foot 4-inch frame cast a shadow that covered the walkway to the house. Feeling his chest start to tighten, he displaced the air in his mouth loudly, sending a shockwave of sound toward Pyrtania Street.

Come on Ross. What the hell are you afraid of? The voice in his head gave him a much-needed pep talk. His chest swelled dramatically as he breathed in the cold night air before exhaling it slowly. Unfortunately, it didn't help for long.

Stories from his adolescent years, about the house that stood ominously before him, caused the hair on the back of his neck to stand up. There was no way of telling whether the chill bumps now racing across his body were from the crisp, southerly winds or from the stories that echoed in his mind, fresh as the day they were told. He searched blindly in the night's blackness for the hole in which the key would fit perfectly. He was rushing to find the keyhole because the hairs standing up on the back of his neck were telling him someone was watching him. He glanced back two or three times, expecting a homeless man to be wandering up the sidewalk. There was no one. He was nearing desperation and full-blown panic when the key finally slid into the antique locking mechanism. Ross took a deep breath and tried to get a good grasp on the key before turning it ever so slightly to the right.

Click.

The echo of the gate unlocking caused the real estate investor to jump slightly. The sound leapt from the gate and wrapped itself around the century old homes on 3rd and Pyrtania, hanging in the thick air suspended heavily over New Orleans. He tried to mentally prepare himself as he let the rusting gate swing unimpeded behind him. The heaviness of the gate slammed itself shut. Ross was now locked in the property and suddenly feeling like a dog trapped in a cage with no chance of an escape. In that instant, he couldn't decide what was more terrifying, being trapped inside the property or standing outside on the sidewalk like a floating target. He stood staring at the marble steps that led up to the large oak door, trying to come up with a reason why this adventure could wait until morning.

When his father, Winston, first mentioned the infamous home was for sale, Ross tried to convince him it would be difficult to renovate and turn a profit in ample time. His father saw right through his smoke screen.

"If you think for one minute I'm going to allow rumors and folklore to keep me from making money, you've lost your damn mind."

Truth was, he knew it would turn a tremendous profit and be successful regardless of the avenue they took. He simply didn't want to spend any more time in the home than he had to. After seeing the home's price tag of only $2.7 million for 10,000-square feet packed with historical artifacts, Winston Hankins knew there was so way in hell they could or would pass up this "bucket list" type of property. The home's 10 bedrooms, 8 bathrooms, servant quarters, carriage house and an appraisal of $9.5 million, it wasn't a deal they could pass. Whether the father-son business team chose to further renovate and resell, or turn it into a bed and breakfast, they were sure to see a return on their investment.

Winston Hankins was one of the first real estate agents in the New Orleans metro area to take up the art of flipping properties. That often meant a full restoration of a historic property or converting an antebellum home into a boutique hotel. Initially these projects were just New Orleans-based and involved small, but worthy projects from Metairie and Kenner. After a few months of successful investments, the father-son duo then set their sights on more profit-friendly properties and eventually started flipping and reselling homes and condos in the Garden District, the Central Business District and even the French Quarter.

Word spread quickly about the business partners, enabling them to expand to the Northshore, south Mississippi and eventually throughout the Southeast. Ross began learning the trade his senior year in high school by going into properties, cleaning them and creating a list of items that were left behind. Eventually, his dad hired him strictly to itemize the contents and price them. Slowly but surely, the strong-willed, now college business major, climbed the ladder until he was his father's right-hand man. By the end of his senior year at Tulane University, he had made enough to pay off all his student loans. Now, a husband and father of twin boys, Ross was his father's biggest supporter, and harshest critic.

Ross' deep breath seemed to reverberate through the empty streets of the Garden District. He thought back to the words his dad had spoken, knowing he was right. The stories were probably all rumors. The severity and truth of the matter had probably been blown so far out of proportion that no one knew what the truth was anymore. He tried to take a deep breath and put the stories and tales behind him, but the more he tried not to think about it, the more it became clear in his mind. Every shadow was a monster of the dark. Each limb blowing in the wind was someone hiding from his view. Even though it was just a little after 8 pm, it might as well have been 4 am. Within a month, these streets would be packed with thousands of party-goers from around the world and locals alike, celebrating Mardi Gras. The massive celebration of indulgence was not something easily explained. The traditional purple, green, and gold colors flowed from the people, beads, and floats like the muddy waters of the Mississippi River. The week-long celebration of parades and parties were not only a way of life for the folks in the South, particularly Mobile and New Orleans, but also a standard part of the Catholic religion. Schools throughout the region closed for a week, as did law firms, doctors' offices, and even multi-million-dollar corporations. It was a holiday as important as Christmas and Thanksgiving, celebrated with more tenacity than a bachelor's party.

The Mardi Gras celebration precedes Lent, when these same partygoers are asked to give up something they desire or enjoy. Many Catholics and other religious folks alike give up alcohol, sweets, or even start a new diet plan that may not have stuck as a New Year's resolution.

Ross stood on the second step and glanced up at the balcony that extended across the second floor of the home and could almost visualize dozens of people manifesting before him, toasting drinks, talking rambunctiously and catching beads being thrown from floats during Krewe of Zulu, Bacchus and Endymion parades. Plastic beads tossed by the thousands from parade participants in every direction, were parade gold, while revelers also prided themselves on collecting plastic cups commemorating the parade, doubloons and even moon pies.

Ross' concentration was shattered by the familiar ringing of the St. Charles Streetcar on the southeast rail, taking folks to

Claiborne Avenue from Canal at Carondelet. Smiling and shaking his head to rid it of past carnival memories and those he could only imagine had happened in this amazing home over the course of its 150-year history.

Ross started his trek up the flowing staircase. The bottom of the staircase fanned out like a calico shell, its rails a least twenty feet apart. However, step by step, the staircase narrowed until the visitor reached the front porch. The design was intended to make guests feel welcomed and invited, but Ross felt anything but that. With each step the foreboding feeling that had settled in his stomach gradually made its way into his throat and chest. Pure claustrophobia overtook his body. He latched onto the cold metal rail on the right side of the staircase, trying to find the stability in it, that he couldn't find in himself. Ross eased his way along the few remaining steps, nearly collapsing as he reached the top. His breathing was shallow and compressed inside his chest. He tried expanding his lungs, but the air seemed to hang onto his ribs, causing immense pain to race through his body before it audibly spilled from his mouth. Before opening the door to whatever lay in wait on the other side, Ross leaned his head back as far as he could, attempting to pull as much of the cold fresh air into his body as possible. He tried his best to regain his composure before making his way to the door.

Placing the end of the flashlight in his mouth and gripping it with his front teeth, Ross fumbled with the keys trying to locate the one that would allow him into the massive estate. He secretly hoped he had somehow left it at the office and would have to come back in daylight hours, but just as a twinge of excitement and hope crept in, he located the gold-colored key.

The lock on the front door was tight and Ross had to put a great deal of pressure on the key before he heard the click and felt the lock give way. As if being ushered in by a long-lost friend, the front door swung open, letting out a high-pitched cry with every inch it moved. Nothing but darkness greeted him on the other side. In pure shock of the grandness of the entryway, he stepped through the front door of the Italianate Neoclassical home. It had been built in 1858 and sported some of the most intricate ironwork ever seen in the city. Its roof even collected rain water, making it the first Garden District home to have an indoor shower. Having been designed by New Orleans native Henry Howard and featured on the silver screen numerous times, the price tag for this massive 10,000 square foot estate easily reached the multi-millions.

Ross nervously took another step into the house, allowing the flashlight to illuminate every darkened corner and bringing life to the furniture that cast eerie shadows throughout the partially lit rooms. A gaudy gold color adorned the walls, ceilings, and even the area rugs and runners that led guests into the body of the home. The constant color made Ross nauseated even though he fully understood that families at the turn of the century didn't want the appearance of their wealth to end at the front door. He made mental notes of what colors should be introduced to the timeworn theme of the home. In the entryway, the old gold would be repainted with a welcoming and sophisticated gray. Deeper inside to the extended hallway which was a major focal point of the house, he noted would transform with a frappe color, sporting a coffee colored trim. Ross looked forward to doing his job every day, but one of his favorite aspects was being able to choose a home's colors. It was amazing how one coat of paint could change the entire look and attitude of a home. This monstrous estate desperately needed a new life and Ross was determined to get it one.

Although the last owners moved out less than eight months ago, Ross couldn't help but feel the home had been empty a lot longer than that. The smells that clung to the interior bordered on mildew, with a slight hint of lavender. There was not an ounce of moisture in the house so Ross had a hard time putting his finger on the source of that particular smell.

According to his father, the last owner simply walked away from the home after only living in it 8 months. From the research he had done at the Orleans Parish Court House, since 1911, there had been no fewer than 21 residents in the home. Ross quickly calculated the average in his head and realized no one was staying more than 5 years, some moving out within just a few months. The last owners, a family of three, simply walked out in the middle of the night. They sent movers for their necessary belongings but surrendered the rest to the estate. What had caused them and so many others to abandon a once-in-a-lifetime opportunity to live in a house so grand? What had they seen? What had they felt? Even though he knew the idea was somewhat far-fetched, maybe, just maybe, the stories about this house weren't rumors after all. He suddenly felt incredibly vulnerable as he stood in the middle of the house with shadow less darkness surrounding him.

A chill rushed over his body as he thought back to the many stories and rumors he had been told about this house through the years. As a high school student at De La Salle, numerous nights were spent cruising the Garden District to Magazine and during each trip a car load of students would stop in front of this house hoping to catch a glimpse of the legend itself. They were certain they had laid eyes on it a time or two, as did the majority of the local teenagers who knew the story by heart. Truth was, Ross always closed his eyes when his friends stopped in front of the house. He didn't want to see a thing this ominous looking house had to offer. When a buddy would say he saw something in one of the top windows, Ross would agree and go along with it until the story died down or until the next time.

Now, he was standing in the foyer of the house that had been the subject of many nightmares not only for him but for the majority of the residents in the New Orleans Metro area. Ross closed his eyes and let out a recondite breath.

"Just take a quick look and come back tomorrow," he encouraged himself as he walked abysmally into the darkness of the house, allowing the house to slowly absorb him. Even though he was only a dozen steps from the front door, he felt as though he were standing at the door of hell.

He felt the deeper he walked into the house, the smaller his chances were of coming out alive or unscathed. With each step he took deeper into the house, he felt as if he were miles away from the front door and his only salvation. He had to consciously make himself take the next step.

His eyes immediately drifted to the gigantic oil painting of Henry Howard, New Orleans' most famous architect, housed in a dark mahogany frame that stood at least 6 feet tall and nearly that wide. Without taking much time to appreciate the painting, Ross was already establishing a price for the sale of the piece. If nobody wanted the painting itself, the frame would easily sell for more than two grand. The last owner left everything in the home including art, silverware, place settings, and furniture, some dating back to when the first owners moved in the home in 1858. That family owned the house until 1911, when the tragedy struck.

Even though it would be a pain in the ass having to get rid of the belongings, the profit from the sale could go directly into renovations and reduce overall costs. Making generalized notes in his head before coming back tomorrow to actually catalog each item, Ross decided the easiest thing to do would be to host an estate auction. With the number of celebrities and Louisiana elite that called the Garden District home, getting rid of the home's items wouldn't be a problem regardless the prices put on them. There may even be a few items the Louisiana Historical Center in Baton Rouge may be interested in, Ross noted.

He reached the massive semi-spiraling staircase on his right and shined his flashlight up to the second floor. Even though Ross couldn't see past the first landing of the stairs, he had the floor planned memorized. The interior balcony on the second floor allowed guests to always know what was going on upstairs or downstairs. Such a rare style for a family home, it was evident to Ross this home was built with only entertaining in mind. As the 10,000 foot home rolled out in front of him, Ross meticulously took inventory while also attaching an attractive price to each item. Tomorrow would be a much easier process since he would already be familiar with each room and item.

After completing the first floor, Ross made his way back to the staircase near the front door. Several times while walking from room to room he was almost certain that someone was lurking in the shadows, memorizing his every move while calculating their next one. Now, as he stood at the bottom of the stairs looking up, his nerves were definitely getting the best of him. There were at least two sharp curves in the staircase, each plunging even further into the dark abyss where Ross was sure evil was waiting, watching, and lurking. Something inside Ross encouraged him to walk the few steps to the front door and return back to the daylight hours. But, another voice overpowered the first one, calling him a wimp, a sissy, and among other things, a pansy ass.

Ross closed his eyes and decided this house and its ridiculous legends weren't getting the best of him today. Plus, how would he explain to his father that a property in the Garden District weirded him out when he had appraised numerous properties in the Low 9th Ward after midnight and didn't think anything about it?

The first step creaked under the weight as he pushed up toward the next one, causing him to pause and listen, as if he was afraid of waking the proverbial monster was hiding in the depths of the house. Ross saw the first landing of the stairs about eight steps ahead of him. With each step up, the pain in his chest and head were almost unbearable. He knew something was waiting for him at the top of the stairs. Once to the landing, Ross sat for a moment to regain his composure and his breath. That's when he heard it. There was no mistaking it now. As clear as the New Orleans sky was that night, Ross knew he heard footsteps on the second floor. The floors were void of any carpet which made each heavy step sound like it was directly on top of him. Ross listened to them come methodically closer to the top of the staircase. It was just a matter of time before he came face to face with the being just a few steps above him. Ross crouched as low to the ground as he could while trying to keep an eye out for the predator. He carefully glanced at the top of the stairs and noticed a figure blacker than black looming over the edge, just above him. Not an ounce of courage or strength remained in the real estate developer as he contemplated his next step. Fear completely overwhelmed the burly investor and the only physical response he had to his present situation was to sit down quietly on the staircase and wait until the intruder had gone or a new wave of bravery invaded his bones. He listened intently as the being seemed to have slowly moved away from the top of the staircase, before backing into one of the many upstairs rooms. Just as the footsteps retreated, the sound of his cell phone ringing exploded through the house, bouncing throughout the empty rooms, causing Ross to jump and emit a strange squeal.

"Oh, shit," he whispered with a mix of fear and anger in his voice.

He couldn't get to his phone quick enough as he dug in his jeans pocket and finally pulled it out. The caller ID said the call was from home

"Hello?" he answered quickly, softly and out of breath.

"Hi honey, when will you be home? I wanted to start working on dinner when you were on the way home," his wife's comforting and calm voice soothed his breathing for a few seconds.

"Uh, it won't be long. Maybe ten more minutes and I'll be headed that way," he answered her, obviously out of breath.

"Are you ok?" She knew something was wrong. His voice was trembling and she could tell he was out of breath.

"Yeah, yeah I'm good. Just working in this house a little," he explained, hoping to satisfy her concern and get off the phone quickly, but realizing his whispering did make him sound suspicious.

"Ok baby, dinner will be waiting on you. Love you!"

"I love you too and I'll see you soon!" Ross hung up the phone quickly and listened for any movements or steps in the pitch-black house. He was not to be disappointed.

The sound of his phone ringing seemed to revive the cloaked figure's efforts in finding Ross and suddenly the heavy footsteps were racing toward the steps in a dead sprint, stopping just inches above where Ross was hidden.

Ross hunkered lower each time as the thought of being seen seemed too much to have to deal with tonight by flashlight. He was certain that the demon was stalking him. Back and forth it paced, as if a hunter was impatiently waiting on his prey to emerge from hiding. Finally, after what seemed like an eternity since the footsteps stopped completely, Ross grabbed the banister and pulled himself up. For an instant he considered bolting down the steps and out the front door.

"It's just my imagination getting the best of me," Ross whispered, trying to convince his heart and mind. After standing and seeing nothing, he resumed his ascent to the second floor.

Having the floor plan practically memorized, Ross mentally established a plan that would get him off the second floor and out of the house as quickly as possible. Without thinking about anything but the task at hand, Ross moved smoothly through each bedroom and bathroom until the only room left was the small office that was a mere ten steps from the top of the staircase. His breathing came easier as he realized he was almost home free.

The office was literally no bigger than a small walk-in closet and besides stacks of Times-Picayune newspapers, nothing stood out to him. Ross was just about to exit the office when his flashlight beam caught the book spine of a novel that looked strikingly familiar.

"Well, I'll be damned," he exclaimed with a smile on his face as he dusted off the front cover, exposing the title and suddenly forgetting he was prey to the shadow in the hall. He flipped the book to its back cover and smiled even more broadly as the image of his old college roommate and best friend smiled back at him.

Dead Moon Rising was the first and only novel by his college roommate and someone he still considered a great friend. Keaton Fordyce was not a name Ross thought of often and spoke of less, but as he stuck the former New York Times best seller under his arm, he vowed to contact him tomorrow. After years of not speaking to him, Ross was eager to catch up with Keaton and see how life was treating the famous author. It was more than three years ago since he had spoken to Keaton and that was while he was on a national book tour that stopped in New Orleans.

With his job complete, Ross couldn't wait to get outside this house. Sure, it would be excellent for business but that didn't mean he had to enjoy being on the premises. The young real estate developer readied his key so he could lock the front door and be on his way without wasting any time.

Ross instantly felt exhilarated as he cleared the first two steps. He paused mid step as a noise behind him sent the hairs on his neck straight up and chills swarming all over his body. His body screamed for him to keep moving but his mind and general curiosity about the home sent him turning on his heels to get a look at whatever was behind him. His eyes attempted to adjust to the darkness in the corners, scanning the entire top floor for whom, or what could have caused the ruckus. Just before turning around and concentrating on the next step on what seemed like an eternal staircase, Ross' flashlight steadied on the wall directly next to the office. He prayed that his eyes and mind were attempting to pull a fast one on him, but he would almost swear he saw movement. Before he had time to train his flashlight elsewhere, Ross' worst nightmare manifested directly in front of him.

Towering over him, the figure, wearing a black cloak with a hood, lunged at Ross. Without a second thought Ross took two steps at a time, hoping his feet would land solidly each time. Within a matter of seconds, the figure was almost on top of him. Ross could feel hot breath on his neck, wrapping itself around his throat, and he expected at any moment to be grabbed and dragged into the hellish depths of the home. When he could clearly see the bottom floor, Ross leapt toward it, automatically skipping six steps. The landing was awkward and the excruciating pain in his right leg caused him to fall to the floor, spilling the objects from his hands. The book slid across the floor and into the formal dining room while the keys slid into the front door. The flashlight struck the floor with a violent, cracking sound before spinning wildly around the home, creating an impromptu strobe light. Ross followed the illumination around the room, looking for his aggressor. There he was standing directly over him, the hood covering everything but his mouth. The figure's lips parted in a mocking smirk and Ross forgot about the injury to his leg and fled the residence, leaving the front door unlocked. He was nauseous as he rushed down the front door steps and onto the sidewalk through the iron gate, allowing it to slam with all its power behind him. Barely stepping off the curb, Ross vomited up everything in his body until all he could do was dry heave. With his nose and eyes running and the remaining acid in his stomach obliterating the lining that was left, he looked back at the house, expecting the figure to be hovering over him. But there was no one there and the Garden District remained just as quiet as it had been upon his arrival.

After collecting himself, Ross began the walk back to his car was parked directly across the street. The sensation of someone watching and following him never ceased. His steps picked up their pace and his neck rotated his head violently as he repeatedly glanced over his shoulders. He hoped his feelings were based on his recent experience or paranoia and nothing more.

Ross collected his thoughts and emotions long enough to get into his vehicle and lock the doors. He sat literally trembling in the front seat for what seemed like hours. He had never been so scared in his life. He had heard about people being frozen in fear and he was incredibly thankful he had been able to move away from the threat. Closing his eyes tight and reaching down to rub his injured leg, Ross couldn't bear to think what would have happened if it had actually caught him. There was now no denying the legend and rumors of this massive estate were indeed true. For now, Ross wanted nothing more than to put this night behind him and get home to his wife and sons.

Chapter Two

THREE HOURS NORTHWEST of New Orleans sits Natchez, Mississippi, hugging the banks of the Mississippi River like it has for thousands of years. Having been settled nearly 300 years ago, Natchez was absolutely the gem of Mississippi. Once the center of commerce for the state and a gateway to the west, some of the most influential politicians in America's history spent time in the riverside city. Its name is from the Native American group that once called its high bluffs and river lowlands home. Now, millions of tourists came through Natchez annually to experience true Old South hospitality, southern soul food, and the hundreds of historic sites that dot the area. Everything Keaton Fordyce ever needed was at his fingertips. However, his days of venturing from his one room flat that sat just a few hundred feet from the Mississippi, were few and far between.

Keaton Fordyce awoke in a panic. The 34-year old moved with the swiftness of a man ten years his junior. The window seemed miles away as he coughed and gagged, begging for a breath of fresh air. He gripped the chipped, partially painted window sill and threw it open. The rush of Mississippi February air into his stale lungs caused him to gasp for more of the pure life giving substance. Keaton leaned as far over the nearly rotten sill as possible and stared down onto River Street, feeling parts of the soft wood crumble under the weight of his hands.

Much like the window sill under his now numb hands, the rest of Keaton's life was crumbling into nothing. Thoughts of his wife and daughter flooded his mind as he watched the mighty Mississippi River flow just outside his apartment, the small breaks in the water shimmered like diamonds in the black mass of water under the full moon. Memories played in his mind unconsciously as he watched New Orleans-bound barges float listlessly down the ancient river. Gradually, as if he were watching a hologram of a movie of his memories, they faded from his mind just as the giant vessels vanished down river.

Keaton allowed half of his body to hang out the one window that contained any sort of view from his apartment. He could feel the weathered, termite infested window sill crumbling beneath his hands. Small splinters of wood began collecting in the dermal layer of his skin but Keaton was too caught up in his thoughts to worry about the pain right now. He couldn't shake the nightmare that had plagued his every slumbering moment for the past week. Dream by dream, more details came to light for him and tonight he had actually awoke in tears. Now, tiny bits of sleet bounced off his face and bare chest as he attempted to gain a fresh breath of air from the cold February night. The ice-laced air plunged into his throat and air canal. Coughing and gagging, Keaton pushed the stale cigarette smoke that clung so tightly to his lungs out into the midnight sky, creating wisps of artificial clouds in the process. A chill violated every inch of Keaton's body as he was plunged back into reality. He shivered as the cold wind caressed his bare arms and wrapped itself around his scruffy face. The slamming of the window against the outside wall echoed through the darkness of River Street. Keaton stumbled back to his dingy, damp, plaid patterned couch. He kicked over empty bottles of Cathead Vodka, creating a temporary path from the window to the couch, less than 10 feet away. Dozens of bottles and empty take-out bags littered his apartment. The only area with any cohesion was the tiny desk that sat in the corner of the living room. There, notes for a future novel were stacked neatly next to his laptop and a single picture of himself with his wife Rebecca and daughter Caroline. He took a deep breath as memories from better days flooded his mind.

He and Rebecca met their junior year at Tulane University. Both being accounting majors, they literally had every class together their junior and senior years and even somehow landed the same internship with Baglio and Hirling CPA's of New Orleans. They married during Christmas break of their senior year and immediately opened their own firm in Natchez following graduation. Nine months later, Caroline Fordyce made her grand entry into the world and their lives were changed forever. The Fordyce's were the epitome of the perfect southern family.

On a Saturday while cleaning up around the house, Rebecca found Keaton's manuscript for the novel he had written while in college, stuffed in a desk drawer. The 314 page dissertation was seductive and tantalizing, and Rebecca couldn't put it down until she had read every last word. The remainder of her afternoon was spent trying to convince him to send it to publishing companies. He finally took her advice and after being denied 9 times, the tenth query came back with a positive response. Almost overnight, the Fordyce's banking account nearly doubled in funds, and that was also when all the trouble began.

Keaton knew he should have never kept any secrets from his wife but he had no idea they would come to light in such a manner. Keaton was the only child of Richard and Mary Fordyce of Natchez. Richard was the Chief Justice of the United States District Court for the Southern District of Mississippi. Politics ran deep in the Fordyce Family, beginning with his great grandfather Shea Fordyce who served as Senator for the 17th District in Louisiana for almost 20 years and his grandfather Milton Fordyce served as the Governor of Louisiana for two terms. There were always jokes passed around at family functions about how politics in the Fordyce Family would end with Keaton. He often thought or hoped he was adopted and wouldn't turn out anything like these other men.

Unfortunately, there was one trait that Keaton inherited in all its brutality. The thought of tarnishing his powerful family's name crossed his mind every day. His grandmother Martha died at the state capital in Baton Rouge several years prior after mysteriously falling down the steps in the main rotunda and breaking her neck. Keaton was sure there was nothing accidental about her death but unfortunately, he never got to prove his theory. By the time he even heard about his grandmother's death, she had already been cremated, without an autopsy. Keaton knew that all mysterious deaths in Mississippi and Louisiana required an autopsy by the state medical examiner. When he brought his concern to his father, he dismissed that his grandfather could have had anything to do with it.

"Your grandmother had been an alcoholic for years, Keaton. Not to mention the numerous pain pills she took daily. Truth be told, she was an addict. There's no telling what was in her system when she came crashing down those steps," his father had tried to explain to him. The last sentence hung on his lips longer because of the smile that had crept across his face.

"That should have been even more reason for grandad to have had an autopsy done. Why was her cremation rushed? She was cremated by the time I knew she was dead," Keaton explained to his father, knowing he would never get the answer he actually wanted.

"The family has an image to keep, son," Keaton's father sternly remarked.

If Keaton had a dollar for every time he had heard that statement in his lifetime, he would be one rich man.

"Well, it's a pretty screwed up image if you ask me," he shot off his response. Sadness, frustration, and anger had taken over his body.

His father stared at him for a few seconds before offering his response.

"Well, nobody asked you; Did they Keaton?"

It was just a few years prior to this death that another tragedy had rocked Keaton's life. His great-grandmother Marilyn died when the car she and Milton were driving hit a tree head on. She was not wearing her seatbelt and he was. Of course, there were no skid marks like the car tried to stop, but who in the hell is going to investigate and doubt the word of the senator? And his mother? She was currently a resident at the Southwest Mississippi Mental Health Complex, suffering from a diagnosis of schizophrenia and manic depression.

Everything Keaton had been told was a lie. All the tragedy his family had been through had been covered in filthy lies usually reserved for the Washington elite. However, great strides had been taken to protect the Fordyce name in Louisiana and Mississippi. He grew up in a home where alcohol flowed as freely as water from the faucet. His father learned from his father who learned from his father and so on. In addition to being damn good politicians, they were also some of the most violent, womanizing men the southern states had ever seen. Coupled with constant alcohol abuse and multiple affairs, the wives never had a chance. In his mind, there was no doubt Martha had been thrown down the stairs; Marilyn murdered in what looked like an accident; and his mom could only take so many blows to the head. In all honesty, Keaton was happy to know she was finally somewhere safe and not at the hands of his father. He knew if she was still at their family home it would be just a matter of time before she was found dead because of some freak accident.

He swore after every beating his mother received for not washing dishes correctly or for not folding clothes a certain way, that he would never be anything like his father and the other men in his family. However, once the money came easy with the book sales and he started touring with Dead Moon Rising, alcohol was everywhere and he wasn't in a position to turn it down. He squandered their money like it grew on trees on everything from the finest of wines to the highest paid escorts. When Rebecca caught on to what was happening, Keaton pulled a gun on her and Caroline and swore they would never leave him. At some point in the wee morning hours he passed out and awoke hours later to a bare house and no family. Now, almost a full year later, he had no contact with them and had no idea where to even start looking if he wanted to. He tried her cell phone around Christmas but no one knew her name. His guess was she was back in Mobile, probably working in her dad's CPA firm. She and Caroline deserved so much better than he could offer anyway so he never tried too hard to find them.

Now, bankrupt, unable to keep a job due to his alcoholism, and no longer working on the book he desperately enjoyed researching, he was living in an apartment paid for by his father for $300 a month. His sole responsibility was the utilities. Most months Keaton would rather have an extra bottle of Cathead than worry about electricity. The only thing he made certain was paid every month was the internet. It was literally his only communication with the outside world. From time to time he would receive emails from publishing companies flirting with him about a new project, while others were from fans of his, begging him to write again. These messages always seemed to come through in the darkest of times, when suicide was a better option than taking another breath or facing another wretched day.

Keaton's memories faded into the 100 year old brick walls like a hologram losing its power source. A chill invaded every inch of his body, causing him to tremble violently, his teeth audibly chattering. He grabbed his Green Wave sweatshirt that barely clung to the back of the broken down plaid couch. He tugged it over his greasy brown hair and freckled shoulders before allowing the middle of the couch to break his unimpeded back first fall.

His eyes swept the floor around the couch, attempting to locate just one bottle with a nice sip of vodka left in it. On the fourth try he found it. The crystal clear bottle with the turquoise cat seemed to smile at him upon his find. Keaton smiled back at the bottle like a long lost friend and in one swift movement, downed the last few ounces of the fluid that had become his lifeblood over the past year.

He felt the Mississippi-born vodka burn his throat on the way to his stomach. He could trace its flow with precision and certainty. A deep, stale breath exited his lungs and Keaton leaned back into the couch.

Keaton stared at the deep coffee colored stains on the ceiling of his one room flat. In the darkness, mixed with the shadows being cast around the room, the outlines of the stains began taking on a life on their own. From island scenes to majestic mountains, Keaton allowed his imagination to run wild for a few brief minutes. He closed his eyes and remembered a time when life was easy and he was actually happy. With the chills finally receding from his body, Keaton slipped off to sleep. Within a few moments, he drifted into a listless slumber.

"Daddy!" screamed Caroline.

Caroline Fordyce, Keaton's four year old daughter, wondered aimlessly around the huge house. She looked even smaller than she actually was as she peeked in every room, desperately looking for someone. The giant doors dwarfed the child who clung tightly to a stuffed pink pig in her left hand.

"Daddy?" she called out, on the verge of tears.

Her tiny voice echoed through the home, being the only sound heard except for the pitter-patter of her bare feet on the ancient wooden floors. Crevices, cracks, sharp sand and even soft spots were sought out by her tiny toes. She could feel the impurities and imperfections with every step she took. From time to time her big toe would be swallowed by a groove in the floor, apparently from where furniture had been dragged across, leaving an eternally deep scar. Besides the darkness and staleness of the home, Caroline could tell that she wasn't alone. The child hung tight to the staircase bannister on the way down the stairs, wrapping her arm nearly around it as she watched her naked feet make contact with the step below her. She heard someone walking on the landing behind her but she didn't turn around.

"Daddy?" she called out again, desperation creeping into her minuet, high pitched voice.

There was no response from the staircase landing, only more footsteps. Heavy, foreboding, and stalking.

With a skip in her step, Caroline rushed to get to the bottom of the staircase. With only one step to go she felt someone grab the bottom hem of her dress. Off balance from the contact, Caroline fell to the hard floor, her knotty little knees striking and then skidding across the slick oak floors. Her thin, delicate skin peeled away from her knee, laying it out in shreds. She could feel the warmth of fresh blood collecting, and then rolling down her legs. Terror and pain overwhelmed her tiny body as she expelled a whimper and bolted towards the front door. Her tiny, trembling hand clutched the brass doorknob with all her might but to her horror, the door wouldn't budge. There was nowhere else to run and feeling the presence of an individual behind her, she turned to face the person with tears now rolling down her face. Her blond ponytail was in disarray and blood had dried to the front of her legs and feet. Caroline swallowed hard in an attempt to subdue the sob that was creeping up on her.

"DADDY!" she screamed as the black-hooded figure in front of her smiled and begin laughing hysterically at her.

Keaton screamed as he awoke from the same nightmare he had just hours earlier. He could not place the home he was dreaming about but somehow there was some familiarity to it, almost a sense of deja vu. His face glistened with sweat as he attempted to process the disgusting dream that had been feasting on his mind all night.

He sat up from the couch and glanced around the room for another bottle of Cathead Vodka or even a bottle of Bluff City Blonde that still had a sip of the spirited beverage inside. Dozens of empty bottles littered the floor and side tables. A partially eaten week old pizza sat just as it did the day he picked it up, minus a few pieces and now crawling with knats and the occasional fly. He used to have it all. A beautiful wife and daughter, a bank account with more than enough in it, and a job as a New York Times best-selling author. He and his family traveled the country for book signings, speaking engagements, and general appearances. Everything was great until he allowed a suppressed demon to rear its ugly head again and take over his life. After sitting back on the couch again Keaton was instantly thrown right back into his dream.

Keaton found himself staring up to the second floor in a house he didn't recognize, nor was he able to coax Caroline to make the journey down the steps again. Instead, she stood silent and motionless at the top of the staircase staring down at him.

"Baby, daddy is right here! Come down the stairs," he yelled up to her, glancing up the stairs and on the open level of the second floor. He wildly searched for the figure that was stalking his innocent daughter just moments earlier.

"Daddy, he's getting closer!" Caroline answered, still in view of her father.

Keaton frantically started climbing the stairs in order to rescue his baby. At each staircase landing he stopped to listen and call for his baby. However, with each step he took, she took one back into the darkest bowels of the house.

"Caroline, daddy is almost up there. Can you tell me where you are?" he cried out. He longed to be able to put his arms around his sweet girl and make sure she was safe with him.

"I'm right here daddy," Caroline answered mordaciously, as if Keaton should have known the entire time.

Shocked as to where the voice was echoing from, Keaton slowly turned around on the third step shy of the second floor and looked toward the foyer on the first floor.

There was Caroline, wearing her favorite yellow summer dress, white flip flops, and a bright yellow bow that shone like the sun on her bleached white hair. It was exactly what she was wearing the last day he saw her. Keaton was shocked to see what appeared to be a spotlight shining down on his daughter in the house that was pitch black. A movement directly behind Caroline made his blood run cold. Due to the illumination of Caroline, he could only see the movement of someone large, standing directly behind her.

Keaton shook his head and closed his eyes in utter confusion. Caroline would have had to pass him on her way downstairs but she never did. Slowly, Keaton started back down the stairs he had just conquered. This time, however, his steps were deliberate and his words calm, as he approached his young daughter and the stranger who stood so closely behind her.

"Caroline, why don't you come help daddy down the last few steps?" Keaton suggested, hoping to pull her further than an arm's length from the dark stranger.

He could tell by the look on her face that she desperately wanted to be away from the stranger in black but there was obviously another force that had taken over her.

Keaton could feel the perspiration collecting on his top lip and brow but his lips felt parched dry. He licked the salty water from his mouth and in turn dampened them. He swallowed hard when he realized he was only 10 feet away from her. However, he chose not to rush in and swoop her up so as to not startle the figure.

"Daddy, you must hurry," the desperation and fear was overwhelmingly clear in her voice now, as her eyes stared straight ahead, afraid to move an inch in any direction.

He watched his feet carefully, not wanting to make eye contact with either of them until the very last moment. His mind was sorting through and contemplating a number of actions and consequences.

When he looked up, he was staring directly into the hooded face of a stranger wearing a black cloak. Besides the arrogant smile that pressed his top lip into his bottom one, no other features of his face could be seen. The remainder of his facial canvas was set too far back in the blackness of the robe. Stepping back after immediately feeling the danger emanating from him, Keaton couldn't lay eyes on Caroline.

"Daddy! Daddy! Daddy!" she screamed, short bursts of sobbing and sniffling in between each time she called out to the only person that had a chance to save her.

Keaton sat up on the couch startled and sweating. His body shivered under his now wet sweatshirt and he looked around the one bedroom flat desperately hoping Caroline was there. Of course she wasn't. He desperately wanted to know the meaning of the dream that had now plagued him for almost a week. Up until this point in the dream however, he had had only been a bystander and not fully involved in the dream. This time when he woke up, he felt for sure he was actually in that house.

He attempted to descramble the thoughts that were racing through his head. He tried desperately to remember each and every detail from his dreams that were getting more and more vivid each night. He walked himself through each moment and made notes on the notepad he kept next to his desk. He had never been in that massive home before but strangely enough, he felt as if he knew the ins and outs of it.

His mind wandered to a time when Keaton felt like he was slowly becoming his father and his grandfather and anybody else that was an alcoholic in his lineage. After all the years of fighting it he finally realized he was in a losing battle. Once graduation had rolled around at Natchez Prep, Keaton packed his belongings and made the 3-hour drive south to New Orleans. With a little over $5,000 to his name from part-time work and graduation money, he rented a room on the campus of Tulane University and got himself a job waiting tables at O'Henry's on Carrolton Street. He didn't care how many 12 hour shifts he had to work, he was never going back to Natchez to live under his father's roof again.

The summer passed quickly and his desire to earn an accounting degree from one of the top business schools in the country was at the top of his agenda. His roommate, and soon-to-be best friend, Ross Hankins was from Kenner and majoring in Real Estate Development and Marketing. The Lexus ES 300 that Ross drove indicated he would be ok, with a degree or not. Come to find out, Hankins Properties had been flipping real estate throughout the south for more than 25 years and now enjoyed a multi-million dollar yearly success.

After Keaton's first experience with Mardi Gras in New Orleans, he started writing a book that had weighed heavy on his mind for a long time but required the perfect setting. In New Orleans he found it. At the beginning of his junior year at Tulane University, the 105,000 word manuscript was completed and printed. On a weekend trip back to Natchez, Keaton placed Dead Moon Rising in a desk drawer and didn't think anything else about it until he had married Rebecca and Caroline had been brought into their lives. Rebecca stumbled upon it when cleaning up their home and harassed Keaton until he submitted it for publication. Nine denials later and Keaton's novel was picked up by one of the largest publishing companies in the country. Almost overnight their bank account increased to levels never seen before. For once, Keaton was not only able to spend quality time with his wife and daughter but he was also finally able to pay off bills that had been nothing but a nag for the last few years. No one but Rebecca knew about the navy blue notebook that Keaton kept locked in his desk. Line after line and page after page Keaton had filled up, almost the entire book, with ideas about future novels. Many of these future projects were already researched completely as well. One novel had lingered in Keaton's mind for many years but he would never be able to write it unless his father was dead. Keaton desperately wanted to write a fictional account of his family, including all the accidental deaths, million dollar checks, and political corruption that seemed to boil over in every election like the flood waters from the Mississippi every spring. However, for now, he would wait on the right time to start a new novel. He knew it was best to wait until his mind was ready write or it would be worthless waste of time.

Keaton's memories took a backseat once he located a cathead bottle with more than a sip left. The teal cat on the clear bottle seemed to beckon him forward and in one swift movement and two gulps all that was left of the honeysuckle flavored brew was the scent.

Even though he once lived a life slightly above middle-class, there was no evidence of it now. After boozing away most of their savings and cheating on Rebecca more times than he could count, she had enough. Hell, he couldn't blame her one bit He felt sick at the thought of allowing his family to walk away without a fight but he didn't deserve them. He deserved a chambered round through his thick skull. Almost on cue, Keaton looked over at the drawer that contained the .38 special. He had bought the 1967 model in a pawn shop in Natchez for a little over $300 to use for protection when he was traveling alone. So far he only had to pull it on one person. This was the one person he could never consider hurting. He kept a box of bullets in the same drawer even though it would only take one to do the job that should have already been done. Slowly, the alcohol in his system changed the channel in his brain and Keaton focused on another aspect of his life. Even though the thought of suicide was fleeting, a day didn't pass that he didn't consider it.

Checking out the time while he glanced at his email inbox on his laptop, he noticed it was only 8:49 pm. He still had a couple of hours before Fat Mama's closed. He slid on a pair of blue jeans and a long sleeve t-shirt he had picked up at the Bonaroo Music and Arts Festival he attended one year in Manchester, Tennessee. He headed out the door for the restaurant two blocks from his apartment. The stinging of the frozen rain falling rapidly now cleared his foggy thoughts quickly. All he could concentrate on now was the Gringo Pie, a fine combination of Fat Mama's world famous tamales drowned in a layer of chili and cheese and adorned with fresh jalapeño slices. Of course, such an amazing meal wouldn't go down without one of Fat Mama's world famous margaritas.

Given the time and the nasty weather, only Keaton and a couple of others were seeking refuge at the restaurant.

Fat Mama's tamales and margaritas were a staple of Natchez life and a favorite among visitors and locals alike. Besides the world famous tamales and knock-you-naked margaritas, the ambience and environment of Fat Mama's was almost as good as their menu selections. One of Keaton's favorite aspects of the restaurant was the mileage pole that greeted all visitors at the back door. It had arrows pointing to a few of the most desirable areas in the world along with mileage to that spot. Keaton never felt he was too far away from anywhere. New Orleans 136 miles. Portland, Oregon - 1931 miles. Edmonton, Canada – 1876 miles. Cancun - 772 miles. One thing was for sure, you couldn't leave Fat Mama's without a smile creeping across your face. The bright yellow interior with decorations you'd only see in a Cheech and Chong movie allowed you to forget about all the troubles of the world, even if it was only temporarily.

"Hey there Keaton," called out Marie, the barmaid who had been a part of the establishment since June 9, 1989, the day Fat Mama's opened for business.

"Hey Mrs. Marie. Kind of a slow night, huh?" Keaton asked as he glanced around at all the empty seats and pulled a chair out from the bar.

Marie had hair as red as the setting sun. It framed her thin face perfectly, the natural locks rolling toward her shoulders like rain water cascading off a boulder after a heavy storm. Keaton never knew her to be married or have any kids, but she wore a diamond band that looked like a wedding band. Even though he had been a regular customer for going on 20 years, Keaton didn't feel comfortable asking such a question. Not tonight anyway.

"Last night was packed but I have to say I'm okay with it being slow tonight. So, what you need tonight friend?" asked Marie, walking in front of where he was sitting, pad and pen poised to take his order.

He had always been drawn to her kindness. He imagined what an amazing mother she would have been. He loved his mother more than life itself but she usually lived her life in an impenetrable haze, thanks to the slew of anti-depressants she consumed like snacks throughout the day. He knew living with his father had been pure hell on her and he was happy she had escaped, even if it was only to a mental asylum.

"I'm going to have the Gringo pie and a margarita," Keaton ordered, never reaching for a menu.

"Jalapeños?"

"Absolutely!"

The older lady winked at Keaton before turning around to get his order to the kitchen.

"So, are you working on a new book?" Marie asked as she placed the Gringo pie topped with a pile of jalapeños in front of the acclaimed writer.

Keaton didn't venture out in the public often but when he did, this was the one question he was always asked, and he always answered it the same way.

"Got a couple of projects I'm working on but nothing in stone yet. Hopefully something concrete by the end of the year," he answered, immediately taking a spoonful of the Gringo pie into his mouth so he could deflect the next question that was bound to come.

Marie smiled and shook her head in approval before moving around the bar to check on the other two guests. She knew his situation and even though he gave the same answer every time, it didn't stop her from asking it.

Keaton honestly wished he had another project in the wings that was ready to be researched. However, he didn't want to do anything anymore. He was perfectly satisfied with sleeping and drinking every day. He had nothing to truly live for since his wife and daughter left, but he also realized staying on this path was not going to get them back anytime soon. In his mind, there was only one reasonable thing left to do.

The small talk with Marie was a nice way to end the night and get his mind off the million other things that had been concerning him.

Just before closing time, Marie walked over to Keaton and hugged him. He was shocked and a little confused.

"Something about the way you're carrying yourself today tells me that you have a lot going on inside that head of yours," Marie started, "and when I'm like that, a hug seems to help a great deal," she finished her explanation with a smile.

Keaton smiled at her and shook his head, having a hard time putting into words what that one small act of kindness had meant to him.

"I absolutely did need that Mrs. Marie. Thank you so much," Keaton finally spoke, a world of emotions spiraling out of control in his head and heart.

That had been the first time he made physical contact with a human since Rebecca left and he had honestly forgotten what it felt like to hold someone close and to actually touch their skin.

Keaton paid for his meal in ones and left a $3 tip for Marie with money that he didn't really have. However, sometimes you have to take chances and help out other people simply because they would do the same thing for you. Keaton began the five minute walk back to his apartment full from dinner and suddenly very sleepy. Even though it continued to sleet, Keaton decided to take the long way home by walking north another block to Canal and then taking a left on Orleans Street. Natchez seemed to already have called it a night, and leaving Keaton with the entire River District to himself.

There had been so many times since Rebecca left that when Keaton would pick a direction and walk. One of his favorite places to be was Natchez Under the Hill when the river was nearing flood stage. There was something dangerous and enticing about being that close to the water with no boundaries to keeping you safe. Keaton's mind wandered here and there and in no time, he was face to face with the beautiful Rosalie Mansion. Ice clung to the white iron fence that encompassed the entire property, keeping unwanted visitors from her immaculate grounds. Keaton got as close to the fence as he could. This enabled him to get the best view of the house, while it was being lit illuminated by the group of floodlights in the front yard.

He always imagined he and Rebecca buying one of these expansive properties. He saw them living out their days watching the Mississippi River from the second floor balcony in rocking chairs, just like some of the first settlers and most important political figures in the state had done two hundred years ago. Even though the incredible estates welcomed millions of visitors each year, Keaton enjoyed learning the dark side of some of these incredible homes.

For instance, Rosalie was built in 1822 by a wealthy cotton broker. However, 95 years prior to construction beginning, the site saw a great deal of bloodshed when the local Natchez Indians butchered the French that were staying at Fort Rosalie.

Also, 41 years after being built, the Civil War came to Natchez. No one was safe from the Union influence, Rosalie included. General Ulysses Grant took over the property and used it as Army Headquarters. Following Grant's reign, General Gresham took over and kept his office on site.

Keaton closed his eyes and rested his chin in-between the ice-cold metal spikes. He tried his hardest to imagine what this area would have looked like during the Civil War and even before then. He desperately wished he could snap his fingers and walk around Natchez during the Civil War, or see just how high the river got during the 1927 flood, or maybe even watch the northern construction workers slave day and night to get Longwood built before the war reached them. Keaton was thankful that even after growing up in Natchez, he never forgot or took for granted the history associated with his hometown. Places like Longwood, Monmouth, Dunleith, and even the Ruins of Windsor just a piece up the river, were not just a part of his childhood but also served as amazing inspiration for the book he published and the hundreds that he kept bottled up in his mind, just waiting for the right time to put them on paper.

His cheeks were red from the cold and his lips starting started to crack from standing in the wind as he gazed and dreamed over the almost 200 year old home. Stepping back on the sidewalk, Keaton started his walk toward the river and then took a left on River Street. If the weather was more conducive, he may have elected to just walk the streets of Natchez all night.

"Maybe tomorrow night will be better," he thought aloud about the idea as he entered his apartment.

Keaton made his way up the rickety steps that led to his second floor one bedroom flat. In different circumstances, his apartment could be a hot commodity. The building that contained the two upstairs living spaces was originally built in 1848 and served as Epstein and Shields Mercantile from 1850-1978. In addition to supplying the clothes and shoes of every school aged child within 20 miles of here during those years, other goods, from caskets to new cars, were shipped up the river from New Orleans. After going out of business in 1978, the building sat vacant until 2009 when a local real estate agent moved her office in downstairs and turned the upstairs into two small flats. With the best views in the city and 165 year old brick walls as your interior, she could easily get $1,000 a month for this prime real estate, but money wasn't a necessity in her life. Keaton had even toyed with the idea that if he ever did get back on his feet that he would fix up the apartment, actually purchase it outright, and rent it out when he wasn't in town. However, looking at his life right now, there was no getting on his feet again.

Chapter Three

IN NEW ORLEANS, midnight was closing in quick on Ross Hankins. However, sleep was the last thing on his mind tonight as he tried to sort out exactly what had happened to him in the Garden District mansion. After returning home and getting everyone comfortably in their beds, Ross searched wildly for a contact number for Keaton. After hours of searching, the only thing he was able to find was an email address he wasn't sure was actually checked anymore.

Ross carefully typed out the words in the email. He had not talked to his old friend in years and had no idea where he even was these days but he needed to reach out to him, especially after finding his book. Ross loved rekindling old friendships and he looked forward to speaking with Keaton. Standing in front of the wall heater Keaton had fired up before leaving for dinner, he watched with great curiosity the small green light blink incessantly on his computer. He knew it was an email and his senses were peaked as he wondered who in the world would be sending him an email at this hour. Not until he could smell his clothing getting hot did he move toward the laptop.

With a slightly hesitant first step, Keaton made his way to the desk and opened his email.

"I'll be damned," he remarked as he saw who the sender was.

He opened the email from Ross Hankins and read each sentence carefully.

Keaton,

Dad and I just purchased an amazing home in the Garden District. Found a copy of your book and decided to reach out to you and see how life was treating you! If this is THE Keaton Fordyce that went to Tulane with me, email me back ASAP.

Keaton sat in the desk chair and read the email over and over again. He hadn't thought of Ross Hankins in months! Keaton wasn't sure how to respond to the email other than being very straightforward with how life was actually treating him.

Ross,

This is Keaton! How the hell are you? Thanks so much for reaching out to me. Life is, well, it could be a lot better. After writing the book, I got in a lot of trouble. I ended up squandering all our money away on drugs, alcohol, and prostitutes. Rebecca and Caroline left me and I'm living in a one room apartment in Natchez trying to figure out the next step in my life. Thank you for reaching out buddy. Maybe we can get together sometime soon!

Keaton hit send and didn't expect another response tonight. Ross was shocked at the outcome of Keaton's life. He seemed to be the one that would always have his life together. He wracked his brain in an effort to find a way to try to help Keaton out of his mess, or give him another chance to get on his feet. Suddenly, he had the perfect idea.

I have an idea that may help you get back on your feet. We're going to renovate the Garden District home starting next week. Why don't you come down and spend some time in the house and see if it inspires you to write a little. You can stay the entire week on a couple of conditions. You bring no alcohol or drugs into the home and once I lock you in, you can't leave until I let you out. We will supply you with all the food and drinks you need. But, I want this experience to not only get you clean but also get you back on your feet professionally too.

My God, a little break would be amazing. Keaton's mind immediately started imagining what this grand New Orleans house might look like. Allowing his imagination to run a little wild, he wondered if this house could help him establish his next novel. As if looking to see if anything was holding him back from agreeing to this proposal, Keaton stood and glanced around the 700 square foot apartment. After nothing pressing jogged his memory, Keaton responded with a resounding yes to Ross.

I would very much appreciate this opportunity and I promise to stay within your conditions as well. Just let me know when to head your way and I will be there.

Like a teenager waiting to be asked to prom, Keaton sat for what seemed like an eternity. Biting his nails and wringing his hands together, Keaton waited on Ross to tell him when to come to New Orleans.

Perfect! Can't wait to see you! If possible, come on down tomorrow morning.

Keaton held his head in his hands. It would be perfectly okay to back out on this invite. One more opportunity to fail is not what Keaton wanted to add to his mental resume. He wasn't sure how in the hell he would be able to make it a week without alcohol but his family deserved his best try.

Keaton stared at the open email, the cursor blinking impatiently, begging for a response. He knew the offer was too good to be true, and no matter how bad he wanted to sober up and start his life over with a clean slate, a nagging, grotty part of him didn't want anything to change. Allowing his tongue to dampen his parched, wind burned lips, Keaton weighed his options on the matter, debating the positive and negative aspects of his decision. The restive cursor begged for attention from Keaton. Coquettish.

With a rebuffed waiver, Keaton's fingers finally typed the words his heart desperately wanted to see but his brain rebuked. In a matter of minutes, plans were finalized and Keaton started packing for his vacation, if you could call it that.

Keaton moved into the tiny bathroom to shave his stubbly face. The integration of brown and gray hair had passed a 5 o'clock shadow days ago. He stroked the chaff with his right fingertips while he glanced over his bare chest. The birthmark directly above his right pec had always intrigued him. Taking his fore finger, Keaton traced the interior and exterior of the indented blemish that looked oddly like a bullet hole. Located just above his heart, his mother had shown the oddity to his family doctor many times through the years, hoping it was nothing to be concerned with. Each time, the doctor assured them it was nothing but a birthmark. From time to time he would mention Keaton was probably a Wild West hero. That general idea stuck with Keaton and even though he knew it wasn't true, he was intrigued with the idea of past lives and if they were actually proper. Even though he grew up Catholic, he wasn't sure where he stood with religion and often times sided with more Wiccan or agnostic beliefs. It wasn't that he didn't believe in God or a god, it was more or less he believed everyone had their own interpretation of their god and believed what they thought they needed to get to Heaven. He had quickly learned while growing up in high society Natchez that not all sins were the same. A teenage girl being pregnant or the star basketball player passing on a scholarship to Ole Miss were talked about much more than the old man that preys on his best friend's daughter.

"Maybe I was Jesse James in my past life," he joked, pulling imaginary pistols from their holsters and pointing them at the man in the mirror, gazing at himself trying to detect the resemblance.

For the first time in what seemed liked months, Keaton was actually excited to welcome a new day into his life. It was the only night he could remember he wasn't praying for his heart to simply stop in the middle of the night. He had nothing to live for these days but the mere thought of possibly starting a new novel had him giddy. Through the years Keaton had absolutely loved and looked forward to the writing process of his novels, on a daily basis. However, now it seemed like the research and collecting of information is what really got his motor going these days. There was a newly found confidence in his step that felt as if it had been years removed, but somehow still familiar.

Keaton packed his suitcase with a variety of clothes. It was the south in February and a 75 degree day followed by a freak snowstorm was not uncommon. Of course a snowstorm in the south usually consisted of less than two inches of accumulation but it was a paralytic experience.

Memories flooded his mind and eyes as he reached for the luggage tag that had been in the exact same spot for over three years now. Southwest flight 1378 from New Orleans to Denver. Rebecca had kept a bucket list since the day they started dating and on top of that list was a visit to the Stanley Hotel in Estes Park. Also known as the Overlook Hotel to Stephen King fans, it had been one of the most fun and romantic trips he and Rebecca had ever taken. They were fortunate enough to drive into Estes Park mere hours before the largest snowstorm of the decade moved and settled over the mountains. For the next four days, the couple ate lavishly in the hotel's famous ballroom, took a ghost tour that made their skin crawl until the sun rose the following morning, and made love like they had during their time at Tulane. Their life had been perfect. Until he decided to squander it all away. They were the epitome of all their married friends and the single ones. A historic tour of Boston and a baseball game at Fenway Park was their next planned destination, but unfortunately their relationship didn't make it long enough to scratch Beantown off their list. Their dreams and goals rushed through his mind in the greatest of details until Keaton had no other choice than to shut the suitcase and call it a night before he no longer felt like going to New Orleans. However, that 3 hour trip south might be one of the best things that could ever happen to him and Keaton swore he would never miss another opportunity presented to him. Crawling onto the couch he had slept on since Rebecca left him, he allowed his body to drift deep into his self-consciousness, unimpeded, and there for the taking.

Keaton almost instantly succumbed to the sleep that was creeping upon him since he had returned from dinner. Almost as quickly, his mind plummeted into a dream, no, a vision of the most violent images he had ever seen.

In his dream he was suddenly transferred to the house he and Rebecca moved into after marrying, the same house Caroline was conceived in. The late, 2-story Victorian model home was built in 1836 and boasted 7 bedrooms and 5 baths among the 6,500 square the massive house encased. Keaton found himself standing just inside the front door noticing all the decorations and paintings of Civil War generals that may or may not have spent some time in it. The ornate, gilded, hand painted ceiling decorations were just as they had been when the Fordyce's called this Natchez jewel home.

The former owner of the home started walking toward the kitchen, being led by the long maroon runner in the middle of the ancient wood flooring. His shoes squeaked on the bare floor once he stepped off the rug, causing Keaton to glance back at the mess he was certain he had made. Squinting to see the first of his steps inside the front door, Keaton couldn't tell if the dark colored, gelatin like substance was mud or... no, there was no way it could be anything else.

"Umm, babe?" he called out to Rebecca, hoping she could offer an explanation as to where he might have tracked in this mystery substance.

He was sweaty in the dream and the knees of his jeans were dirty and worn.

Squatting down at the entryway to the kitchen, Keaton hesitantly stuck his right pinky in the substance that was streaked the entire length of the house now. Glancing at his feet for the first time, he was confused by the large steel toed boots he was wearing.

His pinky broke through the thin mucus layer that had formed over the already coagulated puddle. The thick, rich, life giving substance flowed freely from the tiny nest it had found refuge in for a few brief moments. Keaton studied the bright red liquid on the tip of his finger and could feel panic collecting at his feet and rushing toward his head. Against better judgment, Keaton moved his pinky toward his mouth in an effort to taste the substance. The instant the partial liquid touched the visceral fibers of his tongue, he was completely overwhelmed by the invasion of copper in his mouth, as the thousands of the metallic ions exploded in his mouth. He began trembling violently, causing his chattering teeth to echo through the vacant bottom floor of the home. Now there was no secret as to what the mysterious substance was.

"Rebecca!" he screamed loudly, turning his body wildly in an attempt to catch a glimpse of her, his voice reaching an undiscovered octave.

The home remained silent. But it had transformed around him. Suddenly, a large spiral staircase appeared to his left and the bottom floor was converted into numerous rooms, all serving separate purposes. Formal dining room. Study. Sitting room.

This wasn't the house he and his family had shared for many years. However, that didn't mean it wasn't familiar.

A sick feeling welled up in Keaton's stomach as he quickly realized the house that had just transformed in front of him was the one from all his sickening dreams. In that instant he wasn't sure if he was actually awake or dreaming. This house had intentions for Keaton or he wouldn't be seeing it so often. It was as if the house had come alive in order to consume him.

Keaton, terrified, rushed toward the front door, hoping by retracing his steps, answers about the events of the day would rush back. The outside of the home was normal and manicured just as he remembered their former home being. As he glanced back at the home, the exterior was just as he remembered it.

"What in the hell is going on?" Keaton thought to himself as he frantically started looking for his dear wife.

Suddenly, he remembered the events of the day. When they moved into this home, they were still newlyweds and Caroline had not been born yet.

"What else? What else?" Keaton tried to coax the memories from his mind as he stood on the front steps.

Keaton glanced at his clothing and his hands and noticed a great deal of dirt under his fingernails. He knew instantly the dirt was soil from the flowerbeds and then he remembered. Earlier in the day, they had visited the local plant nursery and decided to plant dozens of tulips around the house. As he started piecing the day together he knew there was only one place Rebecca could be. Keaton hurried around the south side of the house and immediately saw Rebecca's feet sticking out of her tulips.

"No, no, no," he sobbed, knowing in that instant that something was horribly wrong. "Rebecca!" he screamed, tears rolling down his cheeks, collecting with the drainage from his nose to create liquescent as it rolled off his face and onto his shirt.

He rolled her over in an effort to find out how he could help her and was shocked to see one of their own steak knives protruding from her chest. Her beige tank top adorned on the edges with lace, had turned dark, almost black from the amount of blood that had rushed from her body. Images began to collect in his mind like memories of an old black and white movie. He watched himself sneak up on his adoring wife then stab her repeatedly. One. Two. Three stabs to the chest. She never saw it coming and never had the opportunity to defend herself. Her very life blood covered his face. He vomited as he watched himself smile at his now deceased wife before licking his lips clean of the foreign fluid.

Keaton started backing away from the scene that had unfolded before him. He couldn't make himself believe he was responsible for Rebecca's death. He stared at her body for what seemed like an eternity before an image of himself turned and spoke.

"Kinda fun, huh?" he asked, using the back of his hand to wipe more of Rebecca's now dried blood from his face.

With that, he spun away from the body and started running as far and as quickly as he could to get away from whatever he had just done. Just before he reached the corner of the house, Rebecca stepped out into the sunlight.

"Keaton, why would you hurt me and Caroline this way?"

Her words caused Keaton to stumble. He hadn't meant to hurt her and he didn't remember laying his hands on Caroline at all.

"Baby, I don't know what happened. I would never actually hurt you or Caroline," he pleaded with Rebecca through the sobs, his words barely audible.

"Keaton, you can easily say those words but they don't take away this knife in my chest or our baby in that tree," Rebecca responded in a calm, nearly patient way.

"What? What the hell are you talking about Rebecca?" Keaton screamed at his deceased wife that stood just inches from him.

A sadistic smile crossed her face as she slowly pulled the knife out of her chest with one hand and pointed to the large Japanese magnolia that adorned the corner of their lot. Keaton had a hard time taking his eyes of his wife as she held the dripping knife down by her side. He followed the direction in which she was pointing only to see his precious Caroline hanging from the second branch by his belt.

Seeing his baby girl dead, obviously by his hand, he vomited down the front of his shirt. He could feel himself swaying, trying his best not to pass out. At the same time, he wanted to rush to her and try to bring life back to her tiny body but he was frozen in time and slowly started his tumble toward the ground.

Within seconds, he hit the apartment floor with a thud. His eyes immediately found his familiar settings comforting but he couldn't get the images from his dream out of his mind. He could feel himself plunging the knife into her chest. He felt the collapse of her sternum under the pressure of the massive blade and he could feel a sickening excitement creep into his chest.

Glancing at his body wildly, Keaton started breathing a little easier when he noticed there was no blood, no knife, and no dead bodies, and he wasn't wearing the clothes he had on in his dream. He desperately wished he could talk to Rebecca. Needed to. An impossible wish, but a wish nonetheless. Using the couch to brace his body weight, Keaton stood up, dazed and strangely sore. He was surprised to see the early morning sun starting to creep through the only window in his flat. Thinking his nightmare had only lasted a matter of minutes, Keaton knew it had to be at least 7:00 am if the sun was shining so brightly on this freezing Mississippi Sunday morning.

Keaton opened the now stuffy apartment to the frigid air outside. The sleet and rain from the night before seemed to have moved out of the area quickly. Dark gray clouds were parting over the mighty river in order to let the warm sphere break through. The twin spans that stretched from Natchez to Vidalia, Louisiana looked like long skeletal arms made of metal as they ushered the first couple of travelers of the day across the bridge. Fog, thick with crystallized ice pellets, slowly started to lift from the surface of the river, allowing Keaton to see the first barge from New Orleans make its way to a northern port city.

Slowly, bright spectral colors of oranges and yellows cascaded through the sky, appearing to come all the way down to simply touch the earth. Tiny fingerlike bursts of chromatic pink and imperial purple invaded the lowest level, each color contending for the attention of Keaton's eyes. Their hues increased as seconds passed until the large sun was shining proudly for all the early risers to enjoy.

Keaton brushed his teeth and ran his fingers through his greasy, matted hair before double checking the contents of his suitcase. After packing his computer safely away, the hopeful author put the bags in his 1995 Jeep Cherokee. He glanced back at his apartment as if he would never see the building again. Keaton couldn't remember the last time he had taken a trip or had even spent money on gas for that matter. If he needed something in Natchez, he was usually within walking distance. He had gathered up all his loose change and dollar bills he had imprudently tossed into a desk drawer over the past year or so. The $87 dollars in cash and $16 in change made Keaton feel like he had won the lottery. Nothing was going to stop him from getting his life off this runaway train now.

Under the visor on the passenger's side was a single Marlboro. In an effort to simply get rid of the coffin nail, Keaton smoked it down quickly, all while watching the ancient water-based highway fill up with traffic. He tossed the butt of the cigarette into the muddy, churning water below, then made his way to his vehicle.

Nervousness overwhelmed Keaton's body as he climbed into the vehicle for the 3 hour drive southeast to the Big Easy. He knew it was an amazing chance to not only get clean but to also gain traction with a new novel. The possibilities for Keaton Fordyce were endless if he could only keep his head above water and not blow the opportunity that was laid out before him. His life and relationship with his estranged wife and daughter were on the line. Feeling like he had the entire world laid out before him, Keaton climbed into his vehicle and pointed it south. Even though there were numerous ways to get to New Orleans from where he was, Keaton had always been a big fan of staying off the main thoroughfare as much as possible. He always thought travelers along the interstate were sad examples of vacationers because they focused on one thing and drove directly to that point. By taking just one back road, you may not only discover a hidden secret in rural America, but in turn, you may also find yourself.

Driving east along Highway 84, Keaton ushered his vehicle on Highway 98 west, one of the young author's favorite roads. Towering pines and oaks pushed up from the deep crevices on either side of the two lane road, converting the main east/west artery of southwest Mississippi into a shaded break from the hustle and bustle that mostly crowded the highway. Within five minutes of turning onto the major artery that crisscrossed south Mississippi, Keaton crossed the Homochitto River Bridge and into the Homochitto National Forest. Stopping on the side of the road, he climbed out of his jeep and looked into the shallow waters of the river Native Americans referred to as "Big Red River." No deeper than four feet and as clear as the streams that flowed from the most majestic ice-capped mountains, Keaton's mind raced back to the first time he had brought Rebecca home for a weekend. She was a city girl, Houston born and raised and could easily be considered a trust fund baby.

He looked down on the sandbar where evidence of summer and fall bonfires was still engraved darkly into the sand. Burned wood was stacked in piles as if awaiting the return of its campers.

ATV tracks led a way, taking their memories of unforgettable nights with them. His memories flooded his senses as he could remember the first time he brought Rebecca to Mississippi to meet his family. She was a city girl, born and raised in the suburbs of Houston. Keaton had first laid eyes on the blond haired beauty while in Biology his freshman year. Rebecca Mantay was a sophomore accounting major and he was completely and totally smitten the first time he laid eyes on her. The following summer she had agreed to visit Natchez with him for the weekend. They had been dating for about 3 months but besides a quick trip to Mobile and Jackson, they hadn't truly been away together yet.

Keaton smiled as he watched the memories unfold before him. He could see their bonfire burning and their tent set up. Even though Rebecca was a city girl, she was still a far cry from a country girl that would enjoy roughing it on the sand bar of a river overnight. He would have been content fishing all night and walking the sandbar but he realized quickly it wasn't about him. However, he was able to introduce Rebecca to roasted marshmallows, taught her how to bait her hook, and that every noise she heard from the woods wasn't a coyote coming to drag her from the tent to eat her.

Keaton smiled as he remembered how Rebecca snuggled closer to him each time she heard one howl in the distance. He loved her from the instant he saw her but by midnight, he was certain he was in love with her too. That had truly been the best night of his life. He knew the very next morning he wanted to spend the rest of his life with her. His memory, just like the fire that burned in their eyes that night slowly faded away.

A cold wind blew across the Homochitto River, instantly sending Keaton back to his jeep for refuge. A new determination built from deep within him, a feeling he had not experienced in a very long time. He was going to get Rebecca and Caroline back, even if it killed him in the process.

Starting the jeep up, Keaton was overwhelmed with a sense of urgency and excitement. With a new found smile on his face, the author pulled back on Highway 98 and began his track eastward.

Chapter Four

EVERY FEW MILES Keaton would smile when he would lay eyes on an old rural country store that had experienced its heyday many years ago. Gas signs read .89 a gallon and metal signs attached to the front and sides of the painted cinder-blocked building advertised everything from mustard to cigarettes. Keen's Mustard bragged on their 150 year reputation while Wild Woodbine's navy blue signage begged everyone to puff on their strong unfiltered, English-based smokes. The ancient road was adorned by cattle and horse farms and spotted with Mississippi Historical Markers announcing everything from a 1936 World Champion Little League team to the first settlement along Pumpkin Patch Creek in 1812.

Massive oaks stood proudly, nearly hugging the black top while allowing their skeletal arms to reach fully across one lane of the two-way highway. Nine months out of the year the colossal trees shared their canopy of greenery, offering a refuge to anyone willing to take a break from Mississippi's stifling heat.

Keaton was so lost in his thoughts and scenery that he was surprised when the Interstate 55 south exit for New Orleans came up on his right. A slight twinge of nervousness crawled up his throat and into his mouth, causing him to swallow hard. He was pleased to see it was just a little after 8:00 am. Ross wasn't expecting him until 11:00 am and Keaton wanted to wonder around the Garden District a bit before this strange experiment began. He tried to think back to the last time he made this drive and finally settled that it was before a book signing at the Garden District Book Shop in The Rink on Pyrtania Street back in 2013.

The Rink was built in preparation for the 1884 World's Fair in New Orleans and was designed to be just that; a skating rink for the visitors to the city. Now, it was the home of numerous retail stores, an art gallery, book store, and a coffee shop. He had sold close to 250 books in the first hour and signed 500 more on his last visit to the Big Easy. Those were the best days of his life. His fixed smile slowly started to fade into a look of sadness and desperation as the sun hid from view behind graying, heavy clouds, catapulting his good memories to the back of his brain and allowing his negative ones to gain life again.

Keaton, lost in his thoughts, didn't remember driving the 63 miles, but within an hour he found himself in Tangipahoa Parish and the tiny water locked community of Manchac. He couldn't help but think of all the history contained within this tiny water-locked community that had less than 3 miles of actual land in the town. The books written about this area, or the ones that were waiting to be written, couldn't touch even a smidgen of the history and folklore contained here.

One day I'm going to leave here and take all y'all with me.

These were the words of Julie Brown, a self-proclaimed Creole voodoo priestess, who would hauntingly sing from the rocking chair on her front porch in Frenier, Louisiana, just a little ways outside Manchac. In 1915, on the day of Julie's funeral, a hurricane decimated the area, taking everybody attending the graveside service with Julie. Somehow, her prediction had come true.

Louisiana summers are stifling and due to the heat and humidity, the bodies were all buried in a mass grave as quickly as possible to prevent the animals from feasting and diseases from setting in. Anybody that knew where the mass grave was located was long gone now but many adventurers and researchers thought they had not only found that location but also where Julie Brown's house once stood as well. With Julie Brown, the rougarou, and the Cajun werewolf, Manchac had just enough lore to keep authors digging for more.

Manchac sat on the brackish shores of Lake Maurepas, and was intended to be a popular railroad stop along the New Orleans, Jackson, and Great Northern Railroad, but the railroad nor the town ever lived up to expectations of investors and townspeople alike. Besides being home to one of the best fish houses in the south, Middendorf's, Manchac was also home to the ruins of five lighthouses along Lake Pontchartrain.

Keaton could spout information off about Manchac and the surrounding areas almost as easily as he could about his hometown of Natchez. He had more than 500 pages of research about the area in his computer, waiting patiently for his creative hand to indulge itself, turning the dense history and evocative account into a story that would run chills down the spines of anyone brave enough to read it. But like everything else in his life, he put it on the back burner, sure it would be there tomorrow. Or next week. Or even next year. He shelved it all for that "fire water" as his great grandmother had called it many times while scolding the governor himself. All for booze, Keaton thought. He had literally given up everything in his life for a drink. Liquid sin. No different than that found in a Mountain Dew bottle, but a hell of a lot more addictive. He had a hard time making himself believe he was indeed addicted to alcohol. He had tried every drug in the book and even though they were enjoyable, nothing in this world, not even sex with his wife, gave him the same feeling as the liquid libations.

A sweat began to bead up on Keaton's forehead. He wiped it off before it had a chance to roll down his face. He had officially been 7 and a half hours without alcohol. A mere 450 minutes.

Every thought that bounced around in Keaton's head was about alcohol, or the lack of, until Interstate 55 south t-boned Interstate 10. For a brief moment his continual thoughts of alcohol were stalled in order to ensure he took the exit for I-10 east toward New Orleans. He was suddenly excited again. A new found wave of determination seemed to invade his body. Only 30 miles to New Orleans. Thirty miles to salvation.

Traffic was sparse that Sunday morning as Keaton pushed his old jeep almost to its breaking point. He talked kindly to her; he had named her Nicole as he drove it off the lot some 20 years ago. Keaton rubbed her dusty, sun-cracked console, begging her to make one more mile for him. Then another and another. Mile after mile she seemed to get stronger, her gasps, puffs, and near stalls were fewer and farther between.

Finally, Keaton could see the city coming into view. The massive buildings of downtown New Orleans housed everything from world renowned doctors to lawyers that defended the Mafia, a part of New Orleans social and criminal elite for over 100 years.

Keaton knew the Big Easy was a hot bed of ideas for books. From crimes ripped from the headlines on a daily basis to infamous murders and real life characters that have set the world on its ear. No matter where you were in the city, there were stories, rumors, and more than enough information for multiple books.

The city skyline loomed tall and the shadows cast in the early morning light caused the buildings to take on a life of their own. Sunday's were the only days the city wasn't buzzing at 8:00 am. Most of the residents living in the port town were trying to catch up on their sleep, before tackling a busy week of work or partying all over again. New Orleans looked like a post-apocalyptic city as Keaton drove a nearly deserted interstate all while watching the shadows from the buildings creep awake, slowly allowing life within their walls and windows. Singularly entranced by the look of a nearly empty city, Keaton's attention was suddenly captured by a bright blue billboard as he exited onto South Claiborne.

The 35th Annual Crescent City Classic was scheduled for April 19. The 10k was not only one of the fastest in the country but also one of the most popular. With an average of 20,000 running in it every year, it was on every runners' bucket list. When he was younger and 40 pounds lighter Keaton wouldn't miss the event for anything in the world. The bands that played on the neutral ground and the residents that passed beer out to participants on the left side of the street and water on the right, were just a sliver of what he enjoyed about the race. The crazy costumes and the most amazing scenery the Big Easy could offer, added to the camaraderie of the relaxed, fun event. He now laughed at the thought of having to cover the 6.2 miles in one outing. Taking the Claiborne Avenue exit put him face to face with the Mercedes Benz Super Dome, home of the beloved Bayou Boys.

Keaton's mind was overwhelmed with memories from this city that he dearly loved and the times he spent at the dome as a Tulane student. "When the Saints Go Marching In" played loud enough in his mind that he almost started singing along. Washington Avenue quickly came up on this left, causing him to rush back to reality. He was now only a few short blocks from the Garden District. Past St. Charles and Carondelet, Keaton tried to take in all the sights and sounds of the city he had so desperately missed. Within moments, the Lafayette Cemetery appeared to his right and the ever glorious Garden District rolled out before him with multi-million dollar homes saturated with history the owners knew little or nothing about.

Keaton took a left on Pyrtania Street and parked along the right side of the street. Ample parking was a benefit of getting into New Orleans before the tourists and most of the locals awakened from their slumber. The coffee shop in The Rink wasn't open yet so he decided to take a walk through the Lafayette Cemetery. This cemetery had been a favorite place of former New Orleans native Anne Rice and it was rumored she would walk through it during the witching hour, making a concerted effort to communicate with the spirits that called the ancient cemetery home.

The cold February wind ran up one pant leg and down another, sending chills from the bottom of Keaton's feet to the top of his head. He pulled his worn Northface jacket a little tighter around his chest, and walked a block west toward the cemetery. Some of the brightest moments of his tenure in the Crescent City were wandering the streets in the early morning hours. Everything appeared to have a new look, a reimagined meaning, and a clarity rarely seen during other times of the day.

The ancient exterior wall of the cemetery shone through cracked and peeling modern day stucco. The bare brick, which dated back to before the Civil War, had sustained category 5 hurricanes, apocalyptic floods, and the Union soldiers' advancement into New Orleans. Green algae found refuge in the decomposing bricks, each crevice and crack housing the emerald substance, thanks to the infinite dampness that occupied the southern Louisiana air.

The concrete jutted up randomly in front of Keaton, almost causing him to misstep. A colossal friendship oak tree stood proudly and had done so for hundreds of years. Its convoluted root structure stretched hundreds of feet in all directions away from the base. Some running deep and harmlessly under the modern day streets while others violated the brick sidewalk in front of the cemetery. Some sections of sidewalk rose more than a foot up while others seemed to sink under your very step. The more rugged and cracked the concrete was, the more the trees tended to lean toward the middle of the street.

Keaton took the obstacles in stride and stepped from one gray plate to the next effortlessly. As expected, the cemetery didn't open until 10:00 am but that didn't mean he wouldn't be able to get inside. Keaton stood before the rusting barred gate and peered through the small spaces in between. For an instant, the entire world stood still. There were no bells from the local street car, no wind whispering his name through the friendship oaks, no sounds at all except for Keaton's shallow breathing.

"Want me to let you in?" boomed a voice out of nowhere, startling Keaton and causing him to stumble backwards a couple of steps. The peacefulness of the moment was shattered within an instant.

Once his breathing and heart rate were back to normal levels, Keaton cautiously stepped toward the gate again and found a homeless man crouching in the opening of a broken tomb, snuggled closely to the coffin that now jutted out slightly due to the missing faceplate. The young novelist swallowed hard as he could see the gray casket clearly.

"Y..ye...yes..If you don't mind," Keaton stuttered, still wondering why the homeless man had not found a more appropriate home.

Lumbering over like it was such an inconvenience, he pulled a key from his worn denim jacket before swinging the metal gate open loudly. Keaton was sure the opening gate had awakened everyone within ten blocks of the cemetery.

"I take it you're not Johnson C. Derveaux?" Keaton asked the impromptu gate keeper as he opened it just wide enough for the out-of-towner to slide in.

"Hell no. But, he sure provides me a little warmth and shelter on the coldest of nights. I guess you could say, he is quite the roommate," the elderly man laughed aloud, proudly showing Keaton the three teeth that adorned the top row of his mouth.

Keaton giggled, scared to ask any more questions. For a few seconds there was an awkward silence until the old man spoke again.

"I guess you want a tour now too, huh?" asked the man, giving Keaton a sideways looks. "Five dollars will get you the best cemetery tour in the city," the homeless man proclaimed proudly, his chest swelling ever so slightly.

"No, thanks. I know my way around. But, here's a little something for letting me in before regular business hours," he answered, handing him a $5 with a slight laughter in his voice and a grin on his lips he attempted to hide.

"Suit yourself," the elderly man responded, securing his payment in the pocket of his jacket before sitting down on the steps of the tomb he called home.

Keaton began his walk down the main corridor of the cemetery when the old man's voice boomed among the tombs again.

"I know this may be hard to believe, but I'm not on salary here," he stated sarcastically.

Keaton could hardly smother the laugh that was making its way from his throat to his mouth. He coughed in hopes of expelling it.

"Well, the city and tourists are sure missing out! They could at least pay you for ensuring the safety of this place because you sure scared the hell out of me when I heard a voice coming from that grave," Keaton responded with a joke so he could finally unleash the laugher that had built up in his chest.

There was no response from the old man, just a laughter that bounced off the tombs and squeaked with joy for having scared someone. Keaton took a few steps in the cemetery before stopping in his tracks and started glancing around. His eyes desperately searched each shadow and corner hoping there was a news crew recording this experience.

"The shit I get myself into," Keaton mumbled under his breath as he walked away and toward the main intersection of the city of the dead.

Built in 1833 and originally a part of the Livaudis Plantation, it was part of the City of Lafayette until being annexed by New Orleans in 1852. In addition to being the eternal resting place for some of the most famous residents of New Orleans, it had also served as a film mecca to many Grammy-nominated films and the backdrop to literary works about vampires, zombies, and even your everyday murder mystery. There had been rumors about hauntings in the cemetery almost since its conception. Stories ranged from visitors getting guided tours from someone dressed in period clothing to the mysterious hide and go seek ghosts who always seemed to be one step ahead of you, only allowing visitors a quick glance or a shadowed glimpse.

Keaton's first stop was at the Society for the Relief of Destitute Orphan Boys tomb, which had been erected in 1894. As a burial spot for young boys with no family, they ranged in age from 3 months to 9 years old. He knew times were different then, but Keaton had always been interested in knowing how people died.

To be perfectly honest, he had an unhealthy obsession with death itself and often wondered how he would pass. Numerous shelves housed the remains of these young boys who were given an unfair hand to start their young lives. Keaton visualized each child entombed before him, trying to put a fictional face with the names. He imagined each of their stories, where their parents could have been, who these children might have grown up to be. Keaton had a hard time wrapping his mind around the fact that some of these children had lived only a matter of days. Others lived well into their adventurous pre-teens, but were taken down by the flu or yellow fever, or even something as simple as a cough that got out of hand. In his heart, he knew each of these children would have probably lived a long full life had they just been born 50 years later.

At the base of the Orphan Boys Tomb was a large white cross that was covered in pennies. Keaton knew from previous book research that leaving certain coins on graves meant certain things. For instance, a penny left behind meant that the visitor was paying their respect, regardless if they actually knew the dead or not. Nickels and dimes were usually reserved for the graves of veterans. A nickel indicated the visitor had attended basic training with the deceased. However, a dime....well, Keaton had only seen a dime left behind once in all his cemetery touring. A dime meant the visitor was there when that particular veteran made their ultimate sacrifice.

Keaton tried to make an educated guess as to how many pennies had been left behind on this particular tomb. However, the more he looked the more he saw. The copper coins were stacked upon each other in layers that dated back nearly 50 years.

They clung to every crevice and crack in the wall of the tomb as well as the cross. It was humbling to see that thousands of visitors through the years had paid their respect for children they couldn't have ever known. Without hesitating, Keaton dragged the loose change from his pocket and found three of the tawny coins standing out from the silver ones. He started a new layer on the left arm of the concrete cross, stacking the three cent pieces neatly.

Trying to get a better view of the entire tomb, Keaton stepped back a few steps and noticed trinkets he had not seen before. Stacked around the base of the tomb was everything from matchbox vehicles to stuffed animals and Mardi Gras beads. Keaton stood there for a moment, taking in the finality of death and the idea that these young boys probably never knew someone that loved them more than anything during their short lives. Tears welled up in the corners of his eyes as he tried to reason with himself that the Catholic nuns would have shown these children just as much love as any amazing parent. As much as he tried to convince himself of this, there was still something nagging his heart and soul. He couldn't help but think of his sweet daughter and horror overwhelmed his body when he realized she may never truly know him as her father.

Backing away slowly, as if the bodies of the children were about to rise from the tomb, Keaton could feel sweat beginning to collect on his brow and lip and his ears began a high pitched ringing noise that he was certain others could hear. He raised his palms to each side of his head, shielding his ears from voices and wicked screeching that now seemed to be booming, echoing throughout the city of the dead. Making very deliberate steps to ensure he didn't collapse under his own weight, Keaton chose another direction and started walking. His skin was still clammy as he fought to get over whatever spell he had just encountered.

Keaton could literally spend all day in the Lafayette Cemetery if someone was able to tell him the history of every single tomb and person buried there. He had often played with the idea of writing a book along these lines but knew the research would be so incredibly overwhelming that it might actually take away from the idea of the book.

One particular tomb Keaton had always wanted to learn more about was the one lovingly named "The Secret Garden." Even though there is not a lot known about the occupants of the tomb, what is known is a group of friends that were also part of a secret society decided that they wanted to be buried together. These four friends called themselves Quatro and even though there is evidence that a couple were married, they still chose to be buried with their friends rather than their loved ones. Keaton couldn't help but wonder why the men had shared such a closeness or what secrets they were keeping from the rest of the world. Maybe in death was the only time they knew they could trust each other. Unfortunately, any information about their secret meetings, discussions, or anything else the world would like to know now was destroyed by the last remaining member of Quatro. All secrets, notebooks, and ledgers were forever lost to an intentional fire just days before he would join the others in the stark white, above ground tomb.

Keaton opened the notes section on his phone and typed in the names of the men who apparently did many good things for the city of New Orleans during their lives. But, the author in Keaton wanted to know more. He quickly typed Dupuy, Grinder, Palfrey, and Griswold into his phone under the heading of Quatro. He was excited to have a mystery to indulge in. Keaton laughed to himself as he remembered the first time he and Rebecca ever really talked. He was so nervous all he did was spout off a ton of information that she didn't understand about the history of streets, and who was buried where, and why a certain place was called by its name. She smiled kindly and listened to every word as if she was really interested. It was only later that she crowned him the King of Useless Knowledge. Subjects like the ones hidden just out of view in this cemetery were why he started writing to begin with. It wasn't so much the writing but the research that he enjoyed the most. Once he had all the information he needed, he would sit at his laptop, open a vein, and let the book write itself.

Taking a left between the next two tombs led him directly to several tombs called coping tombs. As most people know, due to New Orleans already being below sea level, the water table is extremely high which makes in-ground burials simply not feasible. However, coping tombs allow the deceased to be somewhat buried in the ground if they so desire. A coping wall is built, usually only reaching three feet or so, then the embalmed body is placed into that spot. This is as far down as the dead can be buried without fear of them literally popping out of the ground during the next flood, which happened in several of the major Mississippi River floods and during Hurricane Katrina.

Before leaving, Keaton had one more tomb he wanted to visit that he had not seen in many years. The only iron tomb in the

Brandi Perry | 71

entire cemetery was called the Karstendiek tomb and was the grave that inspired Anne Rice to write Interview with a Vampire. There were a lot of people who wandered cemeteries for inspiration and Keaton was thankful to be gaining similar inspiration as his literary hero.

Trying to keep himself on a schedule so he would have time for lunch before making his way to the address on the note in his pocket, Keaton wandered out of the cemetery, trying to determine if he should head north or south on Washington Street. It had been only 10 hours, or 600 minutes, since he last had a drink. His head pounded and his mouth was parched from the lack of fluids. He needed a good meal and one more drink before he gave his freedom up for the next ten days. Slowly, the familiarity of the Garden District came back to him and he remembered he was only three blocks north of Magazine Street. Any food he could imagine could be found on Magazine, one of the major arteries that connected the Garden District to the French Quarter.

On his walk south he remembered a restaurant he and Rebecca had eaten at on one of their first dates.

"Coquette? Yes, it was Coquette, wasn't it?" Keaton reasoned to himself as he walked past the world-renowned Commander's Palace.

Making the four block walk from the cemetery rather quickly, Keaton was pleased to see there weren't many patrons, being that it was only 10:37 am and brunch had just started. With only $40 in cash to his name, he planned to spend as much as he wanted on one good last meal and drink. For some reason, 10 days felt like a lifetime to him so he better enjoy all the food and drinks, especially drinks, as he could. He didn't have to meet Ross until noon so he had plenty of time to indulge himself for what felt like his proverbial last meal.

Even though everything on the menu looked divine, Keaton couldn't take his eyes off the buffalo apples. Covered in hot sauce, bleu cheese, celery, and walnuts, the combination was a tad bit strange but the idea of the flavors instantly made his mouth water. This plate, coupled with a Sazerac 1850, was sure to satisfy him for the next few hours. He better savor that cognac and absinthe cocktail as long as he could because 10 days was a long time without a drink when you're accustomed to having one every couple of hours. If he could make the 14,400 minutes without alcohol, there's no doubt he would not only be a new man but a new lease on life would be right around the corner as well.

Each bite and sip he ingested, Keaton thought about his sweet family somewhere in Alabama, not giving a second thought to him anymore. As far as he knew, Rebecca may be remarried and Caroline might be calling another man Daddy by now. If so, it was only his fault. Nobody drove them away but him and he was lucky she had not left before. Regardless, the thought still made him sick to his stomach.

Keaton rotated the square ice cubes in his whiskey tumbler at a high rate of speed. They clanked and dinged, and painted the inside of the glass with a thin sheath of frigid water. He put the chilled glass to his mouth and sucked down the last sip of the watered down Sazerac. It was time to get on with the rest of his life.

In fear of having his only mode of transportation towed, Keaton parked in the gravel lot next to The Rink and walked through the Garden District to the house he would be spending the next ten days in. Even though he was certain he had never stepped foot in the house, he knew exactly where it was located. Not once did he attempt to pull the address out of his pocket. Instead, he took step after step in a direction he wasn't sure was correct or not. The only thing he could figure was that he had attended a party there while at Tulane. God knows he and Ross had attended their fair share of parties in their day.

As if he were being led by an internal GPS, Keaton perused block by block before taking a right turn on Third Street. Leaving the address of the deserted home in his pocket, he wanted to see if it was indeed the one he was thinking of.

After a couple of blocks, he saw it. The massive retaining wall was gracefully adorned with century old ivy, only allowing passerby's the opportunity at a teasing, sneak peak of the second floor of the home.

Keaton's mouth gaped open slightly as he walked aimlessly toward the home. He couldn't remember the exact time that he had the pleasure of visiting such a home, but there was no doubt in his mind he had. While standing outside from the front gates of the home, peering at the fanning steps that led to the massive, cherrywood door, Keaton closed his eyes and imagined what lay just beyond the door. He knew there was a partially-spiraling staircase to the right and a long corridor that led to the kitchen and living area. Glancing up at the balcony jutting out from the second floor, he knew the bedrooms were upstairs, each lined against the east wall with the master suite at the very end of the hall. The entire world seemed to be silenced in the moments while he mentally laid out the floor plan of the massive home before him.

"You going to stand there and drool or do you want to come in and actually see the place?" the familiar voice caught Keaton off guard.

Even though it had been over ten years since he had laid eyes on Ross, not one thing had changed about him.

Keaton never heard the heavy door open or Ross walking down the front steps. He was truly in another world.

"Have you been in there watching me the whole time?" Keaton inquired with a grin on his face, as Ross navigated toward the gate to let him in.

"Long enough."

His response didn't require an answer and as soon as the iron gate flew open, Ross embraced Keaton in his massive arms.

"I see you still have the arms of a linebacker," Keaton remarked, trying to catch his breath from what felt like a python squeezing the breath out of his thin, less muscular body.

"Yeah, I work out from time to time," Ross answered, downplaying his two hour daily gym routine. "How the hell are you, man?"

Keaton thought for a moment before he answered the loaded question. Ross noticed the pause and didn't want to press the issue until Keaton was ready to talk.

"Eh, I've been a lot better," Keaton finally answered his question in the most generic way possible, "I have a lot to catch you up on for sure."

Going along with the brief explanation, Ross thought carefully how he would respond.

"Well, maybe this few days away is exactly what you need and maybe it'll even help you get back on your feet."

"I have a couple of book ideas I would like to get laid out so I plan to get a lot of writing done. Regardless if I don't write a word, I appreciate you inviting me down."

"No problem at all. Come on in and see your home for the next few days," Ross stated as he opened the door for his guest.

Keaton stepped in the front door of the massive Garden District Mansion and was instantly welcomed with the warm scent of lavender.

"What a great smell."

Keaton tried to immerse himself in the essential oil by lifting his shoulders slightly and raising his nose toward the ceiling.

Ross sniffed roughly twice and couldn't smell anything but the typical combination of mildew and mold. Taking a couple of steps deeper into the home, Keaton knew exactly where the door on the left went and that there was a secret room under the stairs.

"Did we ever come to a party here or anything?" Keaton asked, knowing he had never stepped foot in this house before.

"Not that I'm aware of but we did party at lot of different places throughout the city," Ross responded, laughing and nudging Keaton with his elbow, as if to recall some of their wilder times.

Keaton wasn't paying attention. He was trying to fight the overwhelming nausea that had taken over his body. He threw his hand over his mouth as a dry heave violently escaped his body. He could hear his sweet Caroline screaming, crying, and calling for him in terror. For an instant, he could see her blond pigtails bouncing as she rushed down the steps of the staircase, trying to escape whatever was chasing her. Just before she reached the bottom step, she disappeared. But what then appeared was even more terrifying. There, spread on the beautiful wooden floors, was the blood from his dream. He kept trying to convince himself that he didn't kill his beloved wife. She and Caroline were safe in Alabama.

Sweat beaded up on Keaton's forehead and his upper lip. The color of his face faded to a weird shade of gray. He could feel his legs becoming weak under the weight of his body and he stretched his right arm out in an effort to grab the wall and hold himself up.

"Hi Keaton."

The trembling, sick author looked straight down the hall and saw the source of all the blood. There, standing just a few feet ahead of him was his wife Rebecca. Impaling her chest was a 10-inch butcher knife, just like what he had seen in his dream.

"Was this one of your fantasies?" she asked him calmly, taking two steps toward him.

Keaton tried to take a deep breath but at that moment the air in the house was as thick as honey. He attempted to answer her, to calm the rage of the wife he never knew to raise her voice.

"If we had stayed would you have murdered us?"

With her question, Rebecca pulled all 10 inches of the bloody knife from her ashen body and her slow walk suddenly turned into an all-out sprint, with the weapon pointed at Keaton.

Keaton was defenseless. All he could do was hold his hands up and beg her not to kill him. Suddenly, the room went black. He could feel himself falling but there was no way to control the landing or the bouncing of his head on the wooden floors.

"Keaton! Oh God, Keaton. Hey, look at me buddy."

The words of his best friend seemed so far away and as if they were being spoken into a barrel.

Slowly, Keaton's eyes opened and he regained his surroundings.

"Shit, dude. What happened?" Ross asked with a terrified look on his face.

"I...I'm not...I'm not sure. Maybe my blood sugar," Keaton could barely get the words out because he didn't know what had happened either.

Ross bolted for the kitchen and returned with an ice cold soda.

"Here, drink this," he squatted next to Keaton and helped him take a couple sips from the soda.

Keaton managed to glance down the foyer and of course there was no blood anywhere. Strangely, the lavender smell was gone as well. It had instead been replaced with the scent of a house that had been shut up for far too long,

"Feeling better?"

Keaton wasn't able to muster up much of a response other than a shake of his head.

"You literally scared the hell out of me," Ross stated, standing up to wipe his own mouth of perspiration.

Keaton scooted on his hands and butt until his back was against the wall.

"I'm sorry, I don't know what happened really. But, I feel better now," he lied, as his skin continued to tingle from the shock of what he saw.

Ross was obviously uncomfortable now. In between scanning the hallway and upstairs foyer, he paced and wrung his hands. His entire demeanor had changed in the matter of just a few seconds. Keaton couldn't help but wonder if he had seen something too.

Attempting to get his legs under him again, Keaton stood up.

"I'm fine now, I promise," Keaton pleaded with Ross, who was now totally uncomfortable with the entire situation, including the house.

"Ok, good. Here, let me show you around real quick and then I will let you go so you can get some rest. You need to get some rest," he stated a few times, attempting to convince Keaton while also trying to find the quickest way out of the house.

Keaton couldn't ignore it anymore.

"Ross, is something wrong?" Keaton stopped the tour of the home abruptly to ask the pressing question.

With a desperate and terrified look on his face, the real estate executive tried to compose himself before speaking any words that would surely expose him more.

"No, no man. You just freaked me out passing out and all and it's got me feeling a little anxious. I'm fine. Everything's fine," he tried to explain away his actions as he walked past Keaton and resumed the tour as if the conversation had never occurred.

"And here is the kitchen. In this refrigerator you have all the food you will need for the next few days. In this one," Ross pointed to a micro fridge in the corner of the kitchen, "is a variety of drinks that you can enjoy. If you run out, check the pantry and load it back up. Everything in this house is yours for the next ten days," he remarked with a nervous smile, constantly glancing over Keaton's shoulder, almost expecting there to be someone else standing there.

Keaton had never seen that much food in one place before. It instantly reminded him of a freezer he would see in a 5-star hotel. He was taken aback by the size of this mansion and couldn't believe he would actually have the run of it for the next week and a half.

As soon as Ross got finished with the tour, he was more than ready to get the hell out of dodge.

"Well buddy, I'm going to leave you to it," Ross stated after a mediocre tour of the house. "Upstairs are just bedrooms and a tiny office. Make yourself at home. Hopefully when I see you again in ten days you'll have a new bestseller manuscript ready to go!" Ross squeezed a smile out of his face and slapped Keaton on the arm, "then we will work on catching up a little more as well. I'll take you to dinner or something, how about that?" The question was a fleeting one as Ross never stopped his route to the front door.

Following him like a puppy, Keaton took every step Ross did until they reached the door. That's when he realized this was the real deal. This journey, or challenge, however he was look at it, was about to begin and Keaton needed to make the best of it.

"I'll see you in a few days! Good luck!"

Keaton stood there, staring out the window at Ross who ran down the front steps, opened the heavy gate and let it slam behind him, all while turning back to look at the home, searching the balcony and windows for something, anything.

"Good luck?" Keaton asked himself, as he watched Ross jog to his car a half a block down 3rd Street, never once taking his eyes off the house.

Keaton turned away from the window and in that instant realized he was locked in this amazing home for ten days. The utter silence in the house made him a little uncomfortable, however.

"What the hell are you hiding in here to scare him so bad?" Keaton yelled from the foyer by the front door, nearly expecting a response.

Of course, the house intended to keep its secrets a little longer.

By now, the late winter sun was trying to squeeze every bit of light it could out of the dimming, almost white sun. Darkness came early in the winter in the south. By 4:30 or 5:00 pm, night would have already encompassed most of the mild southern states. However, during the summer, there may still be a glimmer of light in the sky at 9:00 pm and the sun would rise in all its glory around 5:30 am.

Keaton decided to find the room he wanted to sleep in and unpack the one suitcase he had for the week. He stuck his head in each room of the house cautiously. He couldn't help but think he was a thief in a house of priceless artifacts. Ross couldn't, or wouldn't, explain to him why the previous owners had left in such a hurry they hadn't even bothered to pick up their most expensive collectibles or valued objects. The sofa table in the living room was decorated with a Baccarat crystal case, while every room in the house appeared to have been decorated by Williams-Sonoma's interior design team. Keaton was almost afraid to sit on any of the furniture, much less touch any of the decorative items.

Keaton navigated up the winding staircase to the second floor master suite. The sun was barely making an entrance onto the second floor now. Like the rest of the house, the master bedroom was gaudy, and adorned in gold leaf. The families that lived in this house through the years possessed enormous wealth, and they wanted everyone that came into their home to know it. Personally, Keaton thought every room could use a little makeover and could definitely use a coat of paint here or there to kill the drab look. Until that moment, he couldn't put a finger on what this house reminded him of, but in that instant he knew it was reminiscent of a funeral home. The house, still deathly silent, gave Keaton a sudden chill. He knew the air wasn't on so he wasn't sure where the breeze had come from. He glanced at the French doors on the balcony to make sure they were closed tightly and of course they were.

Attempting to get his mind off the strange feeling he was now having, Keaton laid his suitcase down in the corner of the room closest to the bathroom on a fancy 3-wheeled suitcase pedestal. The porcelain claw foot tub was inviting, but at the moment, the guest of the mansion wanted nothing more than to take a nap on those 800 count Egyptian sheets. Even though he had only been without alcohol for two hours and 38 minutes since lunch, those 158 minutes were beginning to take their toll on him.

Slipping off his blue jeans and tugging his button down shirt off his shoulders, Keaton climbed into the extra-large bed and moaned out loud as the coolness of the delicate sheets seemed to melt around his legs and chest.

"I just need a couple of hours of sleep and I'll be fine," Keaton said to himself just before he fell into a deep slumber.

Chapter Five

BANG! BANG!... BANG! BANG! BANG!

Keaton sat straight up in the bed, trying to shake the cobwebs from his head while also trying to collect his surroundings. It took him several seconds to wrap his mind around where he was. He had not slept that hard in many years and that in itself was enough to disorient him. At that exact moment, he wasn't sure if the loud noise had come from his subconscious or not. He glanced at the clock and noticed it was after midnight. It took several moments for his eyes to adjust to the dark in order to find the doorway, and his mind a little longer to send to send the message to his body to move.

"So much for a little nap," he said out loud to himself, as he threw his feet over the side of the bed.

BANG, BANG, BANG.

Now he knew he wasn't dreaming and the banging on the door was even louder than last time.

"Who the hell could that be at this hour?" he asked himself, trying to peek out the window that faced the street. He couldn't see a thing.

"I bet Ross forgot something," he remarked, finally making it to the doorway.

Unfamiliar with the placement of the light switches, Keaton eased out of the bedroom and, using the walls on either side of the hallway as a guide, his fingers crawling across the surface until he found the staircase in just a matter of seconds.

BANG, BANG, BANG, BANG, BANG.

The beating on the door was louder and angrier than the previous times. Each knock seemed to lift the paintings off the walls before slamming them down again.

"I'm coming! Give me a damn minute!" Keaton yelled as he made his way to the first floor, anger and frustration overriding any fear of who may be standing on the other side of the door, now knowing for absolute certain it wouldn't be Ross.

There, the street lights helped illuminate the foyer. The trombone colored stained glass on either side of the door allowed the shadow of whoever was at the door to cast wildly on the foyer wall. Trying to slow down his beating heart, Keaton took a look at the giant shadow and the silhouette of the person outside and rethought his opening of the door. From where he was standing, it appeared the unnamed visitor was at least seven feet tall. Keaton unlocked the front door quietly and flung it open, expecting a nosey neighbor, or even a drunken college student trying to find the house where all his buddies were. Instead, as he flung the door open, there was no one there. There was no seven foot tall stranger, no nosey neighbor, no college kid. But, he could still hear the repetitious, annoying pounding on the door as it opened, passing him before slamming into the rubber doorstop just inside the home. There, the knocking finally stopped. Keaton stared at the door for a few seconds before he jogged down the steps hoping to catch whoever was playing a joke on him.

"Anyone out here? What kind of joke are you trying to play?" Keaton yelled into the dark night, hoping to scare someone into moving.

The Garden District fell eerily silent and the only thing Keaton heard was his own heavy breathing. He glanced around the enclosed property, staring in the darkest corners while allowing his eyes to adjust to the darkness.

Hearing no one or nothing moving in the brush surrounding the home, Keaton walked out to the gate to see if there was a reason it was unlocked. Grabbing hold of the cold metal with both hands, Keaton jerked it toward him and was a little surprised to find it locked up as tight as when Ross left today. Trying to rationalize the events of the night, Keaton looked along the top of the iron fence that stretched around the property.

Peaking at almost ten feet tall, Keaton knew it was improbable for anyone to be able to climb onto the property simply to knock on the door then flee. He still couldn't get the knocking out of his head and how it continued even when the door was open and it was obvious no one was there.

Keaton held his breath, hoping to hear something in the area that didn't sound right. After a few seconds, he exhaled loudly and turned to walk back into the house.

What he saw instantly stopped Keaton in his tracks. He was so taken aback he lost his balance and stumbled backwards wildly. Chills suddenly covered his body because he was now certain he wasn't the only person on this property. Even though he had not turned one light on while rushing to answer the door, every light in the house was now blazing brightly. A wave of fear swept over Keaton's body as he felt as if eyes were peering at him from every room in the house.

Keaton's head nor body moved an inch but his eyes searched every window, every square pane in the house, trying to understand where this overwhelming feeling of being watched was coming from. There was nothing, or no one in any of the windows on the top floor. But, in the dining room on the first floor, Keaton could have sworn he saw movement in the way of a shadow. As it moved in front of the second window, he was sure of what he was seeing now.

In an instant, Keaton was back in the house and staring into the room he had just seen the figure in. He knew there was no way the person he saw could have disappeared because there were no other exits in the dining room except for the door that leads into the hallway. He couldn't explain it and didn't even know how to try.

Keaton closed the front door but was going to make sure he left all the lights on until daylight at least. Even though it was just the wee hours of the morning, it might as well have been daylight. There was no way Keaton could even think about going to sleep now. His skin continued to crawl and the hair was still standing straight up on the back of his neck. He would do almost anything for a stiff drink right now, even though he knew he was at least nine days away from such a thing. Instead, he did the only thing he knew to do.

Keaton made himself comfortable in the living room and spread his hundreds of pages of research around him. Each stack was designated a single digit, showcased on a bright yellow sticky note. Keaton had them in numerical order based on how he wanted the information to go into his new novel. With his laptop settled in on his lap, Keaton did the next thing he knew best, writing. He didn't remember the last time he was able to even get 1,000 words down before getting up to get another drink out of the refrigerator.

For the first time since Rebecca and Caroline walked out, he didn't feel like his writing was forced. There was nothing to care or worry about for the next nine days, so he was going to concentrate on restarting his writing career and getting his life back on track. If he could survive the lack of alcohol without his body having delirium tremors, going into shock, or lapsing into a coma, he might have a chance to still succeed in this world. Who knows, Rebecca might even be willing to give him another chance.

Keaton leaned his head back and dreamed listlessly off and on as he napped. The laughter of children woke him from a dream about Caroline. With laughter echoing in the background, he woke up with a smile on his face, thinking that he was in the presence of his precious daughter.

Once he was aware of his setting again, he slowly placed his laptop on the coffee table in front of him and eased to the first floor entrance of the staircase, all while looking to the top floor where the giggling was coming from.

"Who's up there?" he asked, feeling a little dumb once the words left his mouth.

He realized there was no way any children could be playing around upstairs.

Keaton rubbed his eyes and forehead, as the first withdrawal headache hit him in between the eyes like an icepick. As he looked at the top of the stairs he was almost certain he saw a shadow of a child run across, but when his eyes were able to refocus through the pain, the child was nowhere to be found. Many times when he was drinking, Keaton felt as though people were playing tricks on him because of some of the things he had seen and heard. One particular culprit was the shadow man that had been seemingly followed him around since he was 17 years old. As a young man, Keaton hoped it was his guardian angel. Now, he was sure it was the Devil himself.

Here however, there was no alcohol in sight and he had been without a drink for a little over 24 hours, or 1,485 minutes to be exact. Therefore, the laughter he was hearing had nothing to do with his addiction.

Taking a couple of steps toward the second floor, Keaton's eyes darted from side to side looking for any movement, intently listening for the next hint of sound.

"Hi there! I'm not here to hurt you. I just want to talk to you. I actually have a daughter myself. About your age," he pleaded with the children, taking another step toward the second floor landing with each statement.

He froze when he heard the bedroom door to the far left creak. Keaton moved his head slightly to get a good look at the door that was slowly opening on its own. Trying to control the giddiness that was building up in his stomach from excitement, Keaton squatted on his heels and faced the door.

"Come on out," Keaton whispered to himself, "come on."

Almost on cue, the door opened the rest of the way and exposed an empty room. However, just as Keaton started to stand up, he heard a noise coming from the room. The closer it got the more familiar the sound was to him.

Keaton squatted back down and was rewarded with a small red ball bouncing out to him. He rolled it back into the room and was pleased to hear laughing coming from what sounded like two young girls. Again, the ball came bouncing out, and again he sent it back into the room, this time his laughter mixing with theirs. However, the game was short lived. Just as the ball entered the bedroom this time, the door slammed with such a force that Keaton could feel the pressure, not to mention the vibration.

The screams that filled the house spilled from the room and sent Keaton reeling. In total and complete fear, he fell backwards before stumbling down the stairs to what he thought was safety below. When his feet hit the bottom, the screams had ceased but the fear and uncertainty about the rest of his stay had not.

Just as Keaton was making his way back to the living room, he heard the bedroom door upstairs creak open again. He quietly but cautiously, walked back to the bottom of the staircase. Keaton tried his best to remain invisible to whoever was upstairs. Even though he didn't want to see or hear anything, curiosity drew him in. Instantly he heard the familiar sound of the ball bouncing again. His eyes finally located it bouncing in place on the second floor landing. Then, as if someone much stronger than a child had palmed the ball, it was flung at it him with such a speed and strength he was almost not able to get out of the way.

As the ball smacked the wall behind his head, it was followed by what sounded like a dozen stampeding men rushing down the stairs toward him.

Keaton made a break for outside, hoping he could keep whatever the hell this was, encased in the home. No sooner than he had stepped outside and closed the door behind him, something slammed into the door so hard that Keaton could feel the door bow out slightly. It was at this very moment Keaton Fordyce realized he was not alone in this Garden District mansion.

Chapter Six

KEATON SAT ON the steps of the century old home for what seemed like hours. He wanted nothing more than to find a way over that fence and disappear for the next few hours. He knew his mind was playing tricks on him but what bothered him most was that at any moment he was just a few feet away from salvation. But he would gladly sit here and take anything the old house had to dish out. The hell that he put his family through was more than he would ever get while detoxing for a week and three days here. Plus, this house and the time here gave him every opportunity he needed to not only get his life back on track but to get another book started. Granted, finishing a book in ten days was nearly impossible unless you were able to knock out 10,000 words a day.

Unfortunately, Keaton had not written 10,000 words total over the last year. He had it in him and lived in the most incredible city in Mississippi, but in the midst of all the sadness and depression, he just couldn't indulge himself like he used to.

Before Rebecca left, the entire family would often spend the day out and about in Natchez. Even though it was his hometown, there was still so much to see and do, and many things you would actually miss on your first visit and not realize it until your second.

The stories associated with the historical homes in Natchez could be worth a book or two all on their own. Longwood was by far Keaton's favorite place to visit, and even though there wasn't a season pass for the house, he paid enough through the years to cover many of these passes. Many times, he went just to gain inspiration from the expansive, beautiful grounds and the exterior of the house. However, the home had a heartbreaking history that he could listen to over and over again.

Initially intended to be five floors and hosting more than 32 rooms, the original planner and owner of the famous octagon shaped house died in 1864, leaving the home incomplete. To Keaton, Longwood was one of the best representations of the Old South. The beauty and strength that it stood for prior to the Civil War continued today, seemingly frozen in time. However, just like much of Natchez and the State of Mississippi, Longwood soon fell into years of disarray.

Just the thought of Longwood made Keaton homesick. He couldn't understand why, though. It had literally been in his back yard his entire life, but in the past year he didn't even attempt to step foot on the luscious grounds.

His daydreams didn't stop with Longwood, though. Instantly, his mind wandered to Dunleith Plantation, Monmouth, Rosalie, and Stanton Hall. Each brought back special memories to him, and he could almost kick himself for not trying to continue to find his interest in these immortal homes. Maybe, if he had been a little more concerned about what was going on around his treasured city and not so concerned with flights to New York, Los Angeles, and Chicago, his Rebecca and Caroline may still be there as well.

Keaton's mind had always gone to the dark side with every writing he ever completed. Part of his first novel brought to light quite a few of the famous hauntings and areas purported to have paranormal experience in the Natchez area. His favorite restaurant other than Fat Mama's Tamales was the King's Tavern on Jefferson.

Built in 1769, King's Tavern was thought to be one of the most haunted locations not only in Natchez but in Mississippi as well. Supposedly haunted by a ghost named Madeline, the mistress of the original owner Richard King, her body, complete with a 19th century dagger, were pulled from one of the walls of the restaurant during renovations just a couple of years back. Owners, workers, and patrons alike, finally had validation to go with some of their stories, regardless of how outlandish they may have seemed at the time.

Many residents of the river city thought the removal and proper burial of her body would bring a close to the continuous activities in and around the King's Tavern, but, to this day, no such thing has occurred.

The memories kept coming and there was no way he could stop smiling or get Rebecca and Caroline off his mind. He couldn't help but remember the days they spent walking the miles and miles of riverfront trails, all while pushing Caroline in her stroller. There were few, if any places that Caroline didn't tag along. She had been on more research trips than most published authors.

The Natchez City Cemetery was another place that could have numerous books written about it. Now that Keaton was out of Natchez and had begun to let his creative genes start flowing again, he was thinking of numerous books he could work on and he enjoyed every minute of it in the process. In addition to wanting to explore the haunted side of Natchez, Keaton had always wanted to write an in-depth history of the ghost town of Rodney, Mississippi. Everywhere he looked in Adams County there seemed to be another idea for a book, whether it was fiction or nonfiction.

There were more than 40 historical markers in the city cemetery but three were so distinct in his mind he couldn't believe the urge to write about them hadn't hit him before today.

The first, and more than likely most famous grave in the cemetery was that of The Turning Angel. This beautiful monument was erected by The Natchez Drug Company in 1908 when their five story building collapsed after a natural gas explosion, killing five female workers, all under the age of 25 with the youngest being 12. The angel that was placed overlooking the graves of the girls is called The Turning Angel because it appears to turn and look at passerby's as they come into the cemetery. Most visitors to the grave are stunned by the sight, while others break down, emotions spreading all over their faces.

Another grave that always seemed to get the best of Keaton was the Florence Irene Ford tomb. After dying in 1871 of yellow fever at the age of ten years old, her mother had two graves dug. One was the grave in which the young girl would spend eternity, the other equipped with concrete stairs. When the coffin was picked out for young Florence, a glass faceplate was installed. Once the stairs were dug, another glass plate was situated between the coffin and the bottom of the stairs. Due to Florence's immense fear of thunderstorms, every time the weather was bad, Mrs. Ford would climb down the steps and sit in the cold, wet, and often dark space, until the weather subsided, so that, even in death, little Florence wouldn't have to be alone.

A very puzzling part of the entire story was the fact that even though Florence was laid to rest in a plot that could easily house 3-4 family members, there is no one else buried in the plot but her. Keaton always had a hard time with this due to the fact that her mother loved her enough to buy and build two graves but yet isn't buried with her daughter. Refusing to go back into the house, Keaton desperately looked around for an old newspaper to jot notes down on. That's when he noticed it. The mailbox was actually on the inside of the gate and the mailman would use a pre-designed hole in the fence to deliver the mail.

Keaton leapt from the steps and rushed to the mailbox, almost begging for there to be junk mail still stored in the metal compartment. He beamed with excitement when he quickly located last week's penny saver and a couple of local coupon books. Anything was better than having to reenter the house.

With this thought in mind, Keaton jotted the girl's name down on the notebook in his lap. He had an aching desire to find out what became of Florence's parents, particularly her mother and where she ended up being buried.

Just a few miles up the road from Natchez was Port Gibson. This ancient little river town also hosted a plethora of exciting historical opportunities to write about. The Ruins of Windsor just might be the most splendid and beautiful home ever completed this side of the Mississippi River. Construction on the magnificent home started in 1859 and was finished in 1861. In addition to slave labor, skilled carpenters and builders were brought in to assume the great task. Even though all the ironwork was shipped down the river from St. Louis, all the bricks used in the home's construction were made on site by slaves.

When the massive, awe-inspiring structure was finally completed, Windsor boasted 25 rooms and 29 of its famous 45-foot brick columns, all at a present day cost of $4.5 million. Unfortunately, the life of Windsor was short lived. Even though it survived the occupation of both the Confederate and Union Troops, it ultimately fell to a guest's cigar in a third floor room.

Keaton made a rough outline of all the places he wanted to visit again and research thoroughly when he made it back to Natchez. As usual, it took getting away to realize what you actually have. This instance was no different.

His mind wandered a little farther to a town he never knew in its prime, only in its disarray and current shape. The town of Rodney is located just outside Port Gibson and had a very storied past. Established in 1828, Rodney first came to fame after only losing the race to be capital of the Mississippi Territory by three votes.

This beautiful ghost town seemingly, in the middle of nowhere was home to one of the most beautiful Presbyterian churches in the state, erected in 1828. Even though the ancient church is still standing, a bruise from its tumultuous past remains. Just above the center window in the church is a 12 pound cannon ball fired into the small town during the Civil War. Even though Rodney wasn't a site of a skirmish, the cannonball was fired into the town after Union officers from the USS Rattler attempted to attend Sunday services. When Confederate soldiers attempted to arrest the officers and hold them as prisoners of war, the firing started.

Although its population never broke 250, Rodney was known as the host for many notable people of the day. Andrew Jackson and Henry Clay were visitors, as was Zachary Taylor, who instantly fell in love with the town. Taylor was so taken by Rodney that he purchased the expansive Cypress Grove Plantation. In addition to its 81 slaves, the cotton and tobacco plantation covered almost 2000 acres. Unfortunately, once Cypress Grove fell into disarray, there was no saving the magnificent home and eventually, it collapsed and fell into the muddy waters of the Mississippi River, leaving only a memory for those left behind.

Daylight slowly started creeping into the Garden District as Keaton jotted down one final idea. He couldn't believe he had sat outside all night and into the early morning hours making notes and transcribing possible book ideas. Back before he was a full-blown alcoholic, he would spend hours on end either on the grounds of Longwood or on a park bench in Bluff Park writing such things. He also realized he had not craved a drink for the short time he had been there either. Had he still been at home, he would have finished off at least a fifth by now. He couldn't believe he was allowing such a thought to cross his mind but he believed in that instance that he was well on his way to the other side of this expansive battlefield. Every step, no matter how small, would be well worth it in the long run. Especially if that meant getting his wife and daughter back.

With each fragment of sunlight that crept into the popular neighborhood, Keaton could literally hear New Orleans awakening from its deep slumber. The first street car bells of the morning rang out with delight and mockingbirds basked in the glow of the morning sun. Within moments, the entire Garden District looked as if it had been white-washed in the blanched light of the new day. Everybody had a chance at a new beginning today and that included Keaton.

Chapter Seven

WITH A RENEWED PURPOSE surrounding Keaton, he decided he would make the rest of this day amazing. There was no way to describe the feeling that had taken over his body other than it being a natural high. With a new found love and understanding for the life he had only been muddling through, it now seemed completely clear. With no fear of what may be hiding inside the house or even just behind the front door, Keaton snatched up all the scraps of paper he made his notes on and headed inside. He wasn't going to let anyone, or anything for that matter, stand in the way of getting his family back.

Keaton rushed into the kitchen and pulled out an ice cold Dr. Pepper, complete with an icy, glass bottle. Clutching his laptop and hundreds of research papers against his chest, he plopped down in one of the large wing backed chairs and settled in for a day of writing. The sobering author multitasked the best he could. With this imaginary bolus pumping adrenaline through his veins, Keaton assumed he better make the best of it. There was a proverbial fire that had been lit in his soul and Keaton knew he had to write until it burned out. Stroke by stroke, letter by letter, Keaton could see his new novel slowly taking shape under his fingertips. He usually didn't know what direction a book was going to go until he started working on it, but one thing was for sure today; he needed to get this story and these words out of his body before they ate him alive.

Keaton wrote to the point of pure exhaustion and once he gave his fingers and mind a break, he realized he was finally hungry. Pulling a Kobe beef steak out of the freezer made him even hungrier. Glancing down at his watch, he was shocked to see that it was only 9:00 am.

"This will need to thaw for two hours before cooking. Gives me time to write a couple thousand words, and while that's cooking I can make the baked potato," Keaton spoke to himself in an effort to have everything in a correct order.

If he had a downfall, it would be the need to have everything in a specific time slot. Even though his life was in shambles, his work and use of time was always a meticulous characteristic. It was easy to say he was OCD, but this disorder didn't affect any aspect of his life except time. Keaton knew he could attribute this to his father.

Keaton sat down at his computer and in that very instant, everything felt right in his world, minus the fact that Rebecca and Caroline were still missing. But, if they could see him now, they would know he was a changed man, changed forever after only a day in solitude. But they couldn't see how well he was doing, nor would they believe his repeated lies of being a changed man. They had heard it one too many times and if he ever got them back it would be on their terms not his.

Shaking his head free from all the cobwebs and memories of the life he once had, Keaton tried to focus on the book he was now obsessively involved in, simply entitled Good Luck Charm. Like many published authors, Keaton would entitle a book something odd just to keep it separated from the rest of the projects he was working on in his mind. He had the idea for the actual working title in the back of his mind but he wouldn't add it until the book figured out which direction it would be written.

He opened his creative vein and let the words bleed all over the paper for the next two hours. Developing characters had always been Keaton's strong point but since he had started writing this one his ability to write in great detail had been especially easy. Each of his characters was based on someone he actually knew, good or bad. He found it much easier to write about the physical attributes of a person he could actually lay eyes on or pull up a picture of rather than attempting to remember all the special details a human can encompass. However, Keaton was sure to never let any of these so-called characters know they were the inspiration for his novel. With every scene he penned, he could almost see, taste, feel, and touch whatever he was describing. So well in fact, he was then able to turn around and place the perfect words for these descriptions.

Just after letting the 3,000th word in two hours slide from his fingers onto the gently oiled keys, it was time to put the steak on to cook. Keaton left the computer open in hopes of writing in between food preparation. Within one minute of typing out his last word, the Wagyu Kobe beef, seasoned with just a dab of extra virgin olive oil and a touch of Tony Chachere's seasoning, was sizzling on the indoor grill. The smell of the near perfect beef was permeating the entire house, causing Keaton to lick his lips in anticipation.

He stood reading what he had written while prepping his loaded baked potato for the microwave. For the first time in many months, Keaton was preparing his own meal and eating like a king this afternoon.

Not only did his soul feel calm and still for the moment, but so did the house. It reminded him of the perfect spring days in Natchez. Keaton stopped and listened for any unordinary sounds. Instead, he was greeted with a deafening silence. He smiled as he sat down to the best meal he had had in years.

He could almost cut the steak with a butter knife and the instant it touched his tongue it started its disintegration. Keaton had never in his life tasted something so exquisite and full of sapidity. The limited, marbled fat wrapped itself around his tongue before exploding into a flavor fit for a king that made Keaton moan.

"Holy shit," he exclaimed, as the first bite of the eight ounce sirloin was gone in just a matter of seconds, with very little chewing effort.

He wanted more and a lot of it. Thankfully, 7.5 ounces remained in front of him. He savored each bite as if he were on death row consuming his last meal. In no time, the rest of the beef was gone. Once he turned his attention to the potato, complete with cheese, sour cream, and bacon bits, it didn't stand a chance either.

When it was all said and done, Keaton was stuffed and could barely hold his eyes open, and it was only 3:00 pm. He dropped the plate in the sink and decided to hammer out a few hundred more words before calling it a night. He was happy with his decision but by 8:00 pm all he wanted was the soft confines of the bed in the master bedroom. He had only been able to enjoy a few hours of teasing, neglectful sleep the night before and Keaton wanted to remedy that tonight. Step by step, be trudged up to the second floor. Having trouble lifting his feet from one step to the next, Keaton could only explain it as being utter exhaustion coupled with food drunkenness. Obviously, the combination was taking its toll on Keaton's body.

Keaton allowed his knees to hit the side of the bed as he took his shoes off and slid them under the edge of the bed. As if he was knocked unconscious, Keaton fell face forward on the bed, allowing the 800 count sheets and down comforter to break his fall, their comforting arms wrapping him in an embrace he didn't care if he ever broke free from. But the chill from the ceiling fan finally got the best of him and in one swift move, he was under the covers and already drifting in and out of sleep. Within 30 seconds, he was gone.

Keaton slept soundly until the sun started creeping into the bedrooms on the west side of the home. He was facing the balcony that covered the entire second floor of the home and the sheer window coverings did little for blocking out the morning sunrise in all her exquisite glory.

With a grunt and a quick roll, Keaton was facing the door with the covers over his head. There was at least a five degree difference from under the covers to the room temperature. This was just the way Keaton liked it. Plunging himself back into total darkness under the covers, he hoped to sleep for at least two more hours. From the stage the sun was in, the 34 year old author could tell it couldn't be any later than 7:00 am, and he had no reason to pull himself out of this cloud-like bed anytime soon.

"Hell no," he said out loud as he attempted to settle back in and go to sleep, shifting his hips to burrow himself deeper into the bed and closer to the foot board.

However, most of the time, whenever Keaton was awakened, he remained that way for the rest of the morning, regardless if it was 3 or 10. Other than writing, he had nothing he had to do today. I mean hell, he was locked in a New Orleans mansion for God's sakes. Being only day three, or 2 ½ depending on who was counting, in the mansion meant Keaton still had a great deal of time to rest, sleep, write, eat, and repeat as much as he wanted to.

Keaton had just slipped into the hypnagogic stage; not exactly asleep, but not awake either, he seemed to be jump roping with the line that made you feel as if you were falling. Several times, he jerked violently, waking himself up, before drifting off again. He was just a couple of seconds away from another deep slumber when a noise in the hallway caused his eyes to pop open and his ears to become more alert and focused. Thinking it was nothing more than the old house settling on the cold morning, Keaton didn't give it much attention until it became incessant.

Trying not a make a lot of noise in order to keep track of the movement, Keaton eased his head out from under the heavy covers and turned his head slightly so that his left ear could hear the noises more clearly. Still, he couldn't yet put his finger on the sound as it echoed like it was 100 miles away even though it was obvious it was on the second floor of the house.

"Thump, thump," Keaton could hear the bumps clearly now and could tell they were definitely making their way down the long hallway to the master bedroom.

Keaton threw the covers back and sat up in bed. Fear caused him to freeze in the warmth of the bed because he knew there was nowhere to go or hide at this point. The closer they came, the easier they were to make out.

"Thump, thump," he could hear the sounds clearly now and there was no way to mistake they were anything but heavy footsteps, and they were headed directly for him.

Keaton could feel his heart rate becoming elevated and his breathing getting more intense. Closing his mouth tightly, he tried to quiet his sudden heavy breaths so as to not be detected and in an effort to keep track of the intruder in the hallway. He knew the steps were slowly but surely closing in on him. Glancing around the room quickly, Keaton realized he had nowhere to go. Sure, he could go out on the balcony but being 20 feet up wouldn't save him from whoever was making their way to the door.

Suddenly, Keaton heard the noise that caused all the hair on his body to stand on end. Like nails on a chalk board, a sick, scraping sound replaced the sound of the boots in the hallway. Chill bumps sporadically started covering the surface of his skin, causing him to shiver.

Keaton moved as quietly as he could to the floor nearest the window and laid flat. From there, he could see the light coming in from under the door, and if someone approached. In just a few seconds, he saw the large boots stop in front of the door.

They ceased, as did the scraping sound. From under the bed, Keaton could see the shininess of something glinting under the door next to the shoes but the half inch crack wouldn't let his vision open up like he desperately wanted it to.

The entire house seemed to hold its collective breath, waiting on the stranger to make its next move. It didn't take long for that to happen.

The copper doorknob rattled a little in its own metallic voice. Even though it was barely audible, the gilded shriek seemed to rattle the stucco and peel the century old paint off the walls. Slowly, the door opened on its own but nobody crossed the threshold. Keaton held his breath for what seemed like forever until the footsteps moved slowly back down the hall.

When he couldn't hear the steps or anything else, Keaton quickly got off his stomach and onto his knees and crawled toward the door. Left open from the unknown intruder, Keaton eased toward it, one hand and knee combination at a time. Everything in his being told him not to look out the door. Slowly, he eased his head out into the hallway and quickly glanced both ways, expecting someone to be waiting around the corner ready to pounce. Surprisingly, the entity had simply disappeared.

Keaton pulled himself off the floor and slowly and quietly made his way downstairs. The first floor looked normal until he walked into the kitchen. There, Keaton witnessed something he could not explain.

There, on the table just as he left it was his computer, still open. The book on the computer had been deleted but the 60 plus pages had been printed out and scattered around the kitchen, many of the pages ripped and others stuck to the walls with water as their adhesive. Keaton hit his knees in defeat.

Chapter Eight

"HOW? HOW IN THE HELL could this happen?" Keaton screamed.

He oscillated between fits of uninhibited rage and the deepest sadness as he saw his latest project, the only one he had enjoyed working on in so long, destroyed and spread all over the kitchen, with no digital file in sight.

With tears rolling from his eyes and his hands still quivering with frustration and anger, Keaton began collecting each of the 66 pages of the manuscript and putting them back together in order.

"What the hell do you want from me?" he screamed at the top of his lungs once he had them all back in place, his eyes and hands raised toward the ceiling as if expecting an answer from a higher power.

There is no anger or frustration experienced like that of an author who had inexplicably lost an entire or partial manuscript. Keaton placed his hands on the top of his head when he also realized all the research he had collected through the years was missing as well. All those trips to research sites, the hours spend in local libraries researching the most miniscule topic, and the money spent to get to and from these locations, money he honestly didn't have. It was all just gone.

Keaton in a frenzy started flinging cabinet doors open, the pantry and refrigerator, hoping there was just one drop of alcohol in the house that the previous owner had left behind and that Ross had maybe overlooked. When it was clear this wouldn't be the case, Keaton came as close as he ever had to completely losing his mind.

The frenzied author dashed from room to room along the first floor of the home, shattering windows, knocking over priceless Ming vases, and even pulling Ziegler Mahal carpet up from the formal dining room. Tears of sadness, frustration, anger, and even desperation, flowed freely from his face. He sobbed aloud and realized this wasn't at all the best decision he had made like he thought yesterday.

"You're trying to kill me! You want me to kill myself don't you? That's what you want isn't it? Here, take me now! Take me out of this hell!" Keaton screamed to whoever was willing to hear.

He clawed at his own neck and wrists in an effort to ease a little of the pain that was pulsing through his body like shards of glass. He thought if he could just fracture the skin a little, it would come spilling out of him like a dam bursting from the pressure of flood waters. All he needed was one little crack to ease his unbearable pain. Keaton fell face first onto the wood floor in the foyer, gasping for air in between sobs but not caring that his saline emotions might stain the century old wood. He didn't want to do anything but die and he welcomed any version of death at that moment. It seemed the entire universe was working together to defeat him and in that instant, he was proudly waving the white flag. Slowly, the entire room started closing in tighter around him until everything went black.

Keaton took one more deep breath, and everything came to a close.

He didn't know how long he had been out but when he awoke again, he was sure it was mid-afternoon. The memories of that morning's fiasco came crashing into his now pulsing head and he was suddenly afraid to look around at the true extent of the damage he had inflicted on the house earlier in the day.

Feeling as if he was coming off a three day high, Keaton slowly pulled himself off the floor to a kneeling position. His head spun with every little movement and his muscles ached as if they had been starved of fluids for several hours. It felt as if Keaton was suffering from one of his classic hangovers but he had not ingested even a single drop of alcohol.

Slowly, he lifted his head, allowing his eyes to make the journey with him. His eyes scanned the room ahead of him and to his surprise, nothing was out of place. Feeling as if he was the star in a new episode of The Twilight Zone, Keaton stood quickly and encompassed the entire main level with unfocused eyes.

"What the?" Keaton summarized as he turned on his heels, trying to find the splattered glass on the floor, the thousand dollar vases in colorful chunks, and the shredded carpet in the dining room.

Nothing. There was nothing out of place or out of the ordinary. Thinking there was some strange possibility that none of those actions ever happened, Keaton rushed into the kitchen to see the outcome of the novel he was working on.

"Oh my God," he exclaimed, exasperated, as he placed the palms of his hands on top of his head.

There in front of him was his laptop, still supporting a brightly lit screen, a cursor blinking incessantly, begging for Keaton to pick back up on the novel where he had left off earlier the prior evening.

Keaton fell into the kitchen chair in a heap in front of his laptop and instantly scrolled through the book, making sure everything was still there.

"64, 65, 66 pages," he counted out loud, each number coming out a little easier than the last.

But something on the last page caught his attention. There was an extra sentence he had not penned himself.

"You've overstayed your welcome here. It's time to leave, Keaton," was all the final sentence said but, in that instant, Keaton knew the truth. He knew he was not alone in this house and he was damned and determined to prove it.

Infuriated by whoever or whatever was playing these sick psychological games, Keaton stood and yelled into the house.

"I'm not going anywhere! You hear me? I'm here to stay!"

And with that, Keaton sat back down at his computer and started hammering out the words to his new novel with a new found emotion and fury both in his heart and mind.

For the next couple of hours, Keaton typed with a frenzy, allowing every emotion in his heart and mind to take over the book. In interviews following the release of his first novel, Dead

Moon Rising, Keaton often claimed he allowed his emotions to write the book.

"I allowed a side of me no one ever gets to experience, to write this book," he was quoted as saying in The Clarion-Ledger newspaper.

This one innocent statement had led critics and fans alike to wonder if Keaton had multiple personalities or some other mental illness. Keaton had scoffed at these claims and never came out with the details of why he cancelled his tour besides personal reasons, which led to even more rumors.

These events played in Keaton's head as he worked diligently on his novel. He paused in the middle of a word and looked up for a moment. He thought back to everything that had happened to him since moving into the home. Was he crazy? Was he finally having the mental breakdown so many others in his family had already experienced? Was he so demented that none of these events were actually occurring, but were just made up by his mind?

Trying to break his train of thought of all the self-doubting ideas, Keaton leapt from his seat and went to the refrigerator to find something to drink. His mouth was dry, parched almost, and made a splatting sound when he opened it wide and licked his lips.

He found the largest cup he could find, at least 22 ounces, and filled it with the hospital-like ice from the freezer. One after another, he poured cans of Dr. Pepper into the cup before taking one hard sip to finish off the last few drops in the third can. As he sipped on the ice cold soda, he rummaged through the side by side, attempting to find something that would quench his insatiable pallet. After his episode this morning, he wasn't certain what time it actually was, but he was hungry regardless of the time.

Pulling out a skewer of shrimp and two frozen stuffed crabs, he was going to pig out again today. The only thing he could think that would make this meal any better would be a bottle or two of Old South Wine. Sweet Noble to be specific.

Keaton licked his lips as he imagined the deep, purple muscadine wine pressed against his lips. He tried to get the thought of the Mississippi-made wine out of his mind by taking another deep gulp of the sugary soda.

The amount of food that was set out on the counter looked as if it was enough to feed the neighborhood. Keaton chuckled at the thought of being a penniless artist, yet eating like a king on a cruise ship. It seemed that no matter how much he ate or drank, there was always more that took its place. He could eat this much five or six times a day and not even put a dent into food that was stored in the refrigerator and freezer.

Just as he placed the shrimp on the grill, Keaton saw what time it actually was and was dumbfounded, the digital clock on the oven read 8:09 pm.

"I was awake by eight this morning, came down here around nine, have been writing for a couple of hours," his voice drifted as the realization of what had occurred that day caused him to go mute. "That means I was passed out on the floor in there for nearly eight hours," his voice drifting off slightly as he tried his hardest to wrap his mind around the idea of being unconscious for that amount of time.

However, it finally made sense to him as to why he was so sore and why he felt as if he was dehydrated. It was because he was. If given the time and opportunity, he would have thought long and hard about what had occurred last night, but thankfully, the sizzling of the shrimp on the grill caused his attention to shift another direction.

Keaton's plate was piled high with grilled shrimp and stuffed crabs as he bounded up the stairs, two at a time, trying to reach the upstairs balcony before starvation gnawed through his stomach. Another tall glass of Dr. Pepper would be used to wash down the briny creatures.

The mid-February night was balmy for this time of year, but perfect for an outdoor dinner. Keaton sat his meal on the table on the balcony just off the master bedroom before placing an old Etta James record on the antique Pyle turntable.

Just as Etta bellowed the first notes of At Last, Keaton took his first bite of stuffed crab. The setting couldn't have been more perfect. He leaned as far back in the plastic garden chair as he could and propped his feet on the inner rails. Beat after beat and bite after bite, Keaton rocked and swayed. Eventually, he was in a state of sub consciousness. He had allowed his mind and body to relax enough that nothing seemed to matter. His head rested on the back of the hard plastic and he was just about to drift off to sleep when he thought he heard his voice being called.

He leapt from his comfortable position and glanced up and down 3rd Street below him, trying to determine if someone was really calling his name or if he was imagining it. Then he saw movement.

"Keaton!" the beautiful blond on the sidewalk below called out.

There she was, standing in an aura of the pale moonlight, Rebecca was calling out to Keaton. Her voice was just as inviting as it always had been and her skin looked so soft, even from the second floor.

Keaton stood up, uncertain if his eyes were playing a trick on him or not. He rubbed them quickly to make sure. He was certain once they refocused that she was going to be gone but she remained on the curb smiling and waving. Keaton allowed his plate to slip from his now nervously damp hands in a state of incertitude. His fresh grilled shrimp bounced freely onto the concrete floor of the balcony.

"Oh my God. Hang on baby! I'm coming down!" he yelled down, not finishing his words before he left the balcony, allowing them to leave a trail behind him.

He truly couldn't believe his eyes. Keaton took the steps in leaps and jumps, two and three at a time until he reached the bottom floor. Rushing to the front door, he flung it open with no inhibitions, expecting to see his Rebecca standing on the other side of the gate. Instead, she was standing face to face with him when he jerked the door open. Her eyes were locked on his the instant he opened the door. Her usual warm smile was now nowhere to be found, but Keaton was too focused on her presence to notice.

"Baby, what are you...?" He started to ask her before she stepped in and placed her mouth on his.

"How did you....?" He broke the passionate kiss only briefly to ask another question. But, again, he started a sentence only to have her interrupt him with a kiss.

To be perfectly honest, he didn't know why she was here nor did he care. All that mattered was that she was standing in front of him and was back in his arms for the moment. He inserted his thumb into the front her jeans and anchored it to the underside of the warmed button, and pulled her close to him. He knew all the buttons to push and was well aware of the responses her body would give in return. This time, he just wanted to return every ounce of passion she was giving him, and to do that, he focused on her neck. If passion is what she came here for, then passion is what she would get.

When his mouth met the soft skin of her neck, he felt her body quiver ever so slightly before the moan erupted from her mouth. She placed both her hands on the top of his head and pulled him in even closer, her body constantly trying to find ways to connect more intimately with his. She pushed her body as close to his as was physically possible, wanting to become one with his for the first time in forever. Nothing else mattered than to be cemented in passion with her husband and Keaton wasn't offering any resistance.

"Take me upstairs," she whispered in his ear, as the petting was quickly escalating to another level.

"My pleasure," he responded with a wide grin, his heart nearly pounding out of his chest.

Taking her by the hand and leading her down the hall to the master bedroom.

Keaton had so many questions for his wife: How did you get here? Where is Caroline? How did you get the gate open? How did you know I was here? Why are you here? But, every time he attempted to ask her one, he was silenced with the power of her kiss or another distracting touch. It was the taste he remembered from the millions of kisses when she was his before, yet there was something different, strange, about this encounter. He tried not to question it too much, he was just so happy she was here. He had missed his wife more than anything in this world. He missed being wanted, being touched.

The trip up the stairs was filled with detours of crawling, clothes pulling, and kissing. Finally, after what seemed like forever, they made it to the bed.

Rebecca shoved him down on the bed with an aggressiveness that he had never seen in her before. Even though it was out of her nature, he wasn't complaining. Keaton finally reached the head of the bed and peered down toward the end to find his wife crawling on all four's on the bed, as if she was about to pounce on her prey.

Her eyes were dark, unmoving. The glimmer he was always used to seeing was nowhere to be found, and neither was the playfulness she usually exhibited in these situations. Rebecca looked almost animalistic, and it turned Keaton on like never before. God. He had ruined his wife.

She licked her lips when she reached his legs, she used her unusually sharp fingernails to pull down his boxer shorts, creating small, jagged, tears in his lower abdomen as a result. With speed and power unrivaled by that of any human, Rebecca was straddling Keaton in a matter of seconds.

The electricity of his body in hers rushed through Keaton like he had never experienced before. His skin literally burned below her touch and he was nearly sent over the edge when he felt her bare thighs tighten on his.

His head flew back in pleasure and his eyes closed. His hands fell from her hips to her upper thighs. But, when he squeezed her legs, all movement stopped.

Confused by whatever had transpired, Keaton sat up on his elbows and opened his eyes. Rebecca sat motionlessly, her hands resting on his abdomen, her head tilted to the right slightly, limp.

"Baby, are you ok?"

There was no response, just her long, sensuous hair hanging near her breasts.

"Baby, what's wrong?" Keaton asked as he reached toward her face to wipe the wisps from her eyes.

Before his hand could reach her face there was a deep, inhuman growl that came from the bowels of his stunning wife. Keaton drew his hand back slowly, carefully, to not spook her.

"Rebecca, I need you to look at me," Keaton pleaded with his wife, unsure if he wanted to see what was on the other side of those blond highlights.

Slowly, her weight shifted back onto her haunches and her hands came off her husband's stomach. The grumbling and growling emitting from the depths of her thin body could be felt vibrating all the way through him. Her head slowly rose off her chest and Keaton started squirming. What he had just got a glimpse of was not his precious wife.

Rebecca's head flew back in such an extreme way that the back of it hit in between her shoulder blades. Her heart beat could be seen bounding through the now thin skin on her taught throat. For an instant, Keaton thought he was going to throw up. Her normally spellbinding emerald green eyes were now as black as the darkest of nights and her face had become drawn at the mouth, creating one thin line where her lips used to be.

"Rebecca," Keaton stated, not sure what he was expecting in response, or if he even wanted one.

In an instant, Rebecca's long nails were buried in Keaton shoulders and her bare chest was laying against his. The contact he had craved only a moment ago now sent tremors of terror through him. The pitch black ovals where her eyes were once housed looked deep into his and leaned even closer. The putrid smell of death encompassed her breath and it seemed to hang on the humid pre-Spring air above the bed. They were now just inches apart.

Keaton knew his opportunities to escape this being were becoming very slim, so it had to be now or never. As quickly as he could, he swung his right arm from his side in an effort to knock her off of him. Instead, with a speed that was unrivaled by any human, she deflected his blow. Her subtle pale white face glowed with rage.

He knew there was no time to try to talk his way out of this so in a last ditch effort he pulled his knees under him and tried to roll her off. Once again, there was nothing he tried that wasn't matched more aggressively on her end. It was evident she was tired of playing with this weakling.

"Oh Keaton, baby, why are you in such a rush," she asked him, her voice shifting from her normal sweet Rebecca voice to that of the darkest of demons. "We were just starting to have fun."

Rebecca threw her head back and cackled a spine-tingling laughter that could only come from the bowels of hell.

The shift in voices truly terrified Keaton. Nothing he could have ever written or imagined would have been even half as terrifying as this moment was.

The demon crawled back up Keaton's body slowly and methodically. He wasn't sure what was going to happen next but he knew it wouldn't be good. The seductive smile that ran across her suddenly voluptuous lips, made Keaton's skin run cold. He was literally frozen in fear.

Using the long, dirty nails to her advantage, the nymph utilized the index and middle finger on her right hand and peeled Keaton's bottom lip back, exposing his close-knit incisors. It didn't take but very little pressure from those nails on the bottom gum for Keaton to cry out in pain and allow his mouth to fly open uninhibited. Putting her left hand to use, she did the same thing to the upper level of his mouth, gaping it open so far that the corners of his mouth became taunt and stretched. He knew the first couple layers of skin were popping and fraying like a strained rope. It wouldn't be long until the rest of the epidermis gave way.

"Keaton, Keaton, Keaton. You should've left when you had the opportunity," the demon spoke again, this time, taking on different voices that ranged from young girls to older men.

Keaton only knew one more thing that could get him out of this predicament.

"Dear.." Keaton started.

"Lord?" the succubus asked, smiling as she realized that she had picked up on his thoughts instantaneously. "Don't you think it's a little too late for him to show up? From the looks of your life, he and everybody else in your life gave up on you years ago," she responded with a giggle that sounded like a response to a teenager's joke, mocking Keaton's effort to call on a higher power.

"Who are you? I demand to know!" Frustration was pushing tears out of Keaton's eyes and desperation was setting in.

Anger had finally taken the place of fear in Keaton's body and he was bound and determined to get some answers before this demon drug him to hell.

"Popobawa!" screamed one voice.

"Trauco and La Fiura!" answered another, its yells overlapping the previous responses.

"Alp," a deep man's voice calmly answered.

"Liderc!"

"Lilu!"

"Incubus and Succubus," the being on top of Keaton wrapped up the roll call. "You see, I can be any one or multiple of these demons at any given time. The thing you should be worried about is which one gets an opportunity with you on the other side first," she commented. Her loud, hideous laughter choked the air out of the entire house before she lunged toward Keaton with her mouth wide open.

Holding steady only a few inches away from Keaton, the demon started sucking every bit of air that his body had created out from his mouth and nose. He tried to cry out as it felt as if each organ was slowly tearing loose from inside his body and escaping from his mouth into her body. Even though it felt like it was taking an eternity, within just a few seconds, the pressure and pain he was experiencing became too great. He could no longer fight everything this house and woman had collectively put him through. He was finished.

"I give up," he whispered.

The entire room went black.

Chapter Nine

KEATON AWOKE many times before daylight, listless, in a subconscious state. Each time he thought for sure there wouldn't be another time of wakefulness because his body ached in ways he had never experienced before. His legs pulsed in pain when they were extended and even more so when bent. His head pounded when he faced the window just as much as when he faced the wall. There was nothing he could do to feel comfortable. For hours on end, Keaton writhed in pain, the only relief coming when he dozed off from pure exhaustion.

Each morning he woke up and gladly counted down each day he had left in the noble home. This particular morning, he wasn't sure if he had been asleep just one day or two, nor did he even know what day it was.

As the sun rose higher and higher in the day, Keaton could not bring himself to move from the bed. He desperately wanted to crawl out from under the sheets and make his way downstairs and to retrieve an ice cold soda. Keaton could almost feel the sensation of locking his lips around the cold, glass bottle and how invigorating it would feel. But, each time he threw the comforter off his body, chills would invade every inch of him, causing him to cover back up in a frenzy. Then, it seemed just moments later, those same sheets were smothering and sticking to him again, causing him to fight his way out to find any relief in the still cold room.

Minutes turned into hours and just before hours turned into more than one day, Keaton jerked himself from the friendly confines of the bed. His feet hit the cold wooden floors and sent a much needed boost throughout him. The room spun around Keaton as he finished pushing the rest of his butt off the bed, forcing his legs to take the brunt of his weight. Two steps toward the door and he finally had the momentum behind him.

Keaton made it into the hallway and was surprised to see it much darker inside the body of the house than he originally believed it to be.

"How long have I been out?" he asked himself, struggling to put one step in front of another and moving with more of a shuffle than a truly defined walk.

Once he reached the steps, Keaton took a deep breath. It would surely take every ounce of his energy to make it down the winding staircase. Using only his right leg, Keaton took a step before bringing his left one to join him, then the right one again. These steps were repeated over and over again until he finally reached the bottom before nearly running into the kitchen to find something cold to drink.

The ice cold soda in the bottle was just as good as he had imagined and even though its coldness burned his throat and nose gulp after gulp, he continued to suck it down until he had to surface for a breath of air. Keaton pressed the enter button on his computer keyboard to get an understanding of what time and day it actually was. He was a little surprised. Even though he felt as if he had slept several days away, he was shocked to discover he was only in the beginning of day five.

"Half way there," he said aloud, shaking his head in amusement, unsure how he had been able to even make it this far, or how he would ever make it to day ten.

Although he could barely muster up the energy to do so, the experiences in this home had piqued his interests and he started pecking away on the keyboard of the laptop, moving quite slowly. There were some days he had to almost beg the words to come, while other days they flowed like they were coming from an open vein straight from his heart. Today, they were there, but his mind and body just weren't moving fast enough to keep up with them.

After only getting 57 words down, Keaton heard the familiar sound of the footsteps again. However, they weren't upstairs as usual. Keaton listened intently as the steps came from just inside the front door and made their way toward the stairs. Even though they were as heavy as usual, they weren't as rushed. Each step was steady, calculated, and had a particular destination in mind.

Keaton moved away from the computer toward the entryway to see if he could actually lay eyes on the trespasser. Of course there was no one there. However, he was able to mentally follow the footsteps up the staircase, where the steps paused briefly before taking a left and then a right into the first bedroom. The footsteps stopped there and Keaton was instantly drawn toward the steps.

As quietly as he could maneuver, he tiptoed over to the bottom of the steps, hoping to hear anything at all that was going on upstairs with his ghosts. Residual hauntings is what he had started calling them. There was no other way to describe them. They always seemed to repeat the same course every time. He had imagined there must be several spirits that still remained on the grounds. Undoubtedly, this house had produced some of the best times for the families that called this estate theirs.

Keaton lifted his right leg to start his way up the staircase when he heard a sound he had not heard before. He placed it back at ground level and turned his head slightly in an effort to gather as much of the sound as possible. The house seemed to hold its breath as Keaton listened. A misplaced scraping sound took the place of the footsteps momentarily. Keaton was puzzled, to say the least and started up the stairs to find the cause of the new, abrupt sound.

The early, quiet morning hours in the home were suddenly interrupted by the screams of a young child coming from the same room. Every piece of glass in the house seemed to quiver under the shrillness of the screams that were emitting from the upstairs room. Keaton took the steps two at a time but he knew no matter how fast he went there was no way he could stop the horror that was going on in there.

He tried to prepare himself for the grotesque site he was sure to see on the other side of that door but when he threw the door open, he was stunned to see nothing, no one was there. Keaton sat down on the twin bed for a few seconds and tried to collect his thoughts and settle his rapid heart.

Chapter Ten

AFTER AN INCREDIBLY PRODUCTIVE day of writing, Keaton turned in to bed early to listen to the early spring showers fall over The Big Easy. Leaving the balcony doors open, the heavy showers pelted the tin roof, creating a lullaby that is not easily reproduced. Keaton faced the open doors and allowed the cool southerly wind to embrace his face and bare arms. Not wanting to ruin the paradise-like sounds that filled the air around him, Keaton just slid further down under the heavy comforter. Within just a few more minutes, his heavy lids were no longer able to pop back open on cue at every little sound in the house. He allowed his now nearly sober self to enjoy the slumber.

For the first time in many nights, the sleep not only came quickly, but heavy as well. Keaton hoped this only meant he was getting back into some of his old, normal, routines. Rebecca used to tell him the world could end around him and he would never know it. However, once alcohol became the focal point of his life, sober was hard to find and the sleep that was found was light and restless. Even though Keaton looked for every tiny bit of evidence to prove his life was slowly becoming normal again, he was almost certain the amazing sleep he was experiencing here was from many extrinsic factors. In addition to the absence of alcohol, this house was warm and free of drafts and dampness, unlike his flat back home. Since being here, he had not been exposed to the suicidal thoughts and tendencies he had his last few days in Natchez. Even though he couldn't begin to explain half the events that occurred in the house thus far, Keaton simply chalked them up to alcohol withdrawals. He knew from his hours of research on the matter what to expect. The first step would be rigors and chills, followed by audible hallucinations. If that wasn't terrifying enough, the third phase brought on visual hallucinations, and finally a complete mental breakdown.

After sleeping for what felt like hours, Keaton was awakened by a sound. He laid in the dark for a few moments, unsure if the sound had actually occurred or was part of a subconscious dream. Stifling his breathing for a few seconds, he listened to see if the noise repeated itself from outside the open balcony doors.

It didn't.

However, just as he was about to close his eyes again, he heard it. He couldn't believe he hadn't recognized the sound before. Originally, the sound he heard had to be that of the door knob to the bedroom moving ever so slightly. But, there was no mistaking the second one, which was the sound of his bedroom door creaking open.

Keaton desperately wanted to gasp for air in an effort to calm his suppressed breathing and raised heart rate which had both become quite erratic when he realized what the noises were. Instead, he shifted himself slightly in the bed so he could get a good view of the door. Keaton felt like his lungs were going to explode and his heart was going to beat out of his chest. He was sure by now the intruder could hear it beating in his chest like an empty tomb. Sure enough, the once closed door was now standing slightly open, and he was certain his hiding place had been sold.

The frightened tenant begged for his eyes to adjust to the light enough so he could see who was standing just beyond the door in the shadows.

"Come on, come on," he whispered to himself, straining his eyes, almost sure that he was starting to make out the image of someone standing in the door.

As the door started to swing open even further, he was certain whoever was at the door could hear him swallowing repeatedly in an effort to calm the rest of his nervous body. Keaton tried to swallow the thumps that had crawled into his throat but to no avail.

There it was. The lights on 3rd Street provided just enough illumination to the second floor room that the entire body of the intruder could be seen. Even though Keaton could make out the outline of the person perfectly, he had a hard time making out what the individual was holding in his right hand, but there was obviously an object there.

Keaton searched the room with his eyes, looking for anything he could use to defend himself against this intruder, whose intent was obviously violence. Before he had a chance to decide on a particular object, the being was only steps from the bed and was starting to lift the mystery object up to his side.

Rolling on his back in the best defensive position he could think of at the moment, Keaton lifted his hands above his head as the stranger brought the object down with force onto the bed, barely missing Keaton's head.

"Why are you doing this? Please, take whatever you want!" he screamed at the intruder as he realized there was an 8-inch axe blade imbedded in the mattress next to him.

As snow white feathers danced throughout the room, the weapon was retrieved from the bed by the intruder, Keaton rolled out of the way and toward the floor to get away from the barrage. He glanced at the clock as he rolled off the bed, searching for cover from the maniac who had invaded his room.

3:07 am

The instant Keaton's body hit the floor, his eyes flew open. He looked around the room carefully and cautiously, searching for the feet of the intruder while also trying to determine his next move.

Now, the bedside clock read 3:06 am.

That's when Keaton heard it. The unmistakable sound of the doorknob being turned as quietly as possible. Pewter doorknobs make a particular sound when tampered with and there was no way Keaton was going to mistake it twice. On cue, the door creaked open, leaving the black void of the hallway behind it, the hiding place of the axe-wielding maniac.

Keaton had to act now if he was going to survive. As quickly and quietly as he could, the author now drenched with sweat, slid off the bed on the side nearest to the windows. He attempted to slide under the bed but his wet clothes and body screeched against the wooden floor, causing him to freeze in fear of being found out.

He was sure the sound had echoed through the house the same way it had bounced off his eardrums but, as he laid still and peeked under the bed for confirmation, there was no movement from the door. Keaton rolled onto his belly, faced the door and waited. There was nothing else to do.

The room remained as still as the Lafayette Cemetery for what seemed like ages until Keaton heard movement on the bed above him.

"Baby, I thought you closed the bedroom door," the woman's voice stated.

"I did," responded the man, the sureness responding in his voice.

Keaton reached down the side of his bare leg and jerked a couple of course hairs out by the root. The pain jolted him slightly but he could still hear the voices above him. It was suddenly very clear to him, he wasn't dreaming.

There was no response from the lady again, only the audible gasp of her voice as she realized someone was entering into their bedroom.

"Jack, there's someone at the door," she whispered to whom Keaton could only imagine was her husband.

"What?"

Confused and disoriented, Jack, as she called him, couldn't put together in the dead of night that there was actually an intruder in their affluent home.

This time, with her voice a little more shrill and panicked, she spoke again.

"Jack! Wake up! Jack!"

Keaton felt chill bumps crawl all over his body. He knew exactly what was about to happen next and there was nothing he could do about it. She had finally seen the outline of his body come through the door and she also saw the object in his hand, even though she had no idea of what it was at the time. He couldn't wrap his mind around what he was experiencing, but the weight of the mattress just above him proved to him it was very real.

"Who are you? What are you doing here?" yelled Jack into the darkness, finally awake enough to see the man invading his bedroom.

There was no response from the individual who was dressed in what appeared to be a black robe complete with a hood, moving toward the bed with a mission and murder in mind.

"Please stop him," pleaded the young wife to her husband, now moving closer to him on the bed.

The husband spoke again. This time, anger had given way to fear and his words were mixed with tears.

"Please. You don't have to do this."

But, no matter how much pleading and crying were set before the intruder, his footsteps never slowed, never wavered.

"Please don't hurt my babies!" the mother screamed as she saw the glimmer of the blade flying towards the bed at a remarkable and unhindered speed.

Keaton heard the steel blade strike the mattress with a thump. The sound it made over and over again as it rained on their skulls, arms, and legs were unmistakable. The shrill cries of terror were mixed with the disgusting sound of splitting skulls and the shattering of other bones in the body. The screams eventually turned to whimpers and those eventually faded to moans, then silence.

Continuing to hold his hand over his own mouth in an attempt to stifle his cries, Keaton shook in fear and shock of what he had just witnessed. After a few tense moments, the murderer was done gazing at his handiwork and walked out of the room. Keaton continued to lay there for several seconds, until blood began oozing through the mattress and dripping on his face. Keaton choked back the vomit that came rushing up from his stomach into his throat. He immediately threw his hands over his mouth in an attempt to lessen the pressure that was collecting behind the putrid liquid.

In a frenzy, Keaton rushed from underneath the bed, attempting not to look at the terrible spectacle that lay sprawled across the top of his hiding place. Down the hall he went, now concerned with stopping the massacre of the children at the end of the hall. Even though the hallway was only 40 feet long Keaton felt as if it was one step forward and three steps back.

He stepped in the doorway of the children's room and was horrified to see the cloaked figure standing next to the bed with the axe raised high. The sun was barely coming through the window, only allowing the silhouette of the children to be seen as bumps in the bed. The fringe of their small sleep hats stuck out slightly. They were unaware their tiny lives were hanging in the balance.

"No!"

Keaton screamed as loud as he could, hoping that some way, somehow, his voice and emotions would break the continuous loop of history that kept repeating itself. Of course, it didn't change a thing and within a matter of seconds, the screams of the two young girls boomed through the house, dropping Keaton to his knees while tears rolled from his eyes.

He was broken, helpless, and wanted to walk away from everything this house represented. He couldn't make sense of what it all meant yet but he knew this house held secrets that were ugly, horrible, and downright evil.

Keaton finally pulled himself off the floor in the hallway. A quick glance into the kid's room told him exactly what he thought. It was residual. Everything was just as it was 30 minutes ago. The bed was made, the curtains were pulled, and there was no sign of blood or carnage around. Zapped of all emotion and strength, Keaton moved back toward the master bedroom to confirm exactly what he knew he would find.

Sure enough, nothing but an unmade bed met him there, where he had been asleep just a few moments ago. The balcony doors still stood open, inviting the cool, damp February air to permeate the second floor of the home. Dejected and an emotional wreck, Keaton made his way downstairs somehow determined to start the day. There was no way in hell he would be able to sleep anymore that was for sure.

Even though he only had four days left in the Garden District, Keaton was bound and determined to find out the secrets of this house and leave it more peaceful than he found it.

Chapter Eleven

KEATON SHOULD HAVE been ecstatic to escape from this self-imposed hell but he simply didn't have the energy. It had been at least two days since he had eaten anything. As the activity in the home increased his appetite had taken a tumble, as had his willpower to make it through the last couple of days. But he had a plan for tonight. If the hooded figure returned again tonight like he had the previous two nights, he was going to intervene. At this point, Keaton would rather run himself into the rusted edge of that axe than watch the massacre unfold again. And again. And again. Tonight, one of two things would happen. The murders would stop, or Keaton would die trying.

Keaton had been sitting in the same chair since the previous night's events, pecking out every emotion, frustration, and guilt-stricken element to what he was experiencing in the house. The lack of food and sleep were definitely taking a toll on him but at least he was getting a book written.

Struggling to move due to lack of sleep and nutrition, Keaton decided he had to make an attempt on this day even though he wanted nothing more than to find a way out of this hell hole.

Keaton had fallen asleep at the kitchen table where he had written diligently for the past 22 hours. Fueled by no sleep and even less food, he listened intently for the nightly rituals to start upstairs. Keaton tapped each letter of the keyboard striking it with a cadence only found by drummers in a marching band. The sounds the letters made bouncing off the walls were nearly as loud.

He couldn't believe in just nine short days here he had been able to hammer out nearly 300 pages of a brand new book. Right now, it was more or less just ramblings of incoherent thoughts of his days here. However, his beta readers who were spread out all over the country from Seattle to Atlanta, were able to turn this jumbled pile of words from an ant hill to a gold mine in only a months' time. He wasn't worried. His job right now was to just get his thoughts down on paper and that's exactly what he was doing. A thousand words here, a hundred more here, 5000 there, and before long, he was looking at a full manuscript.

In between each paragraph, Keaton would pause and raise his glance toward the ceiling of the kitchen in an effort to coax out the sounds and apparitions that had appeared night after night for the past two evenings. Besides the normal bumps and creaks hosted by the ancient home, there was nothing amiss. However, just as Keaton started on a new chapter, there was a noise upstairs that caught his attention. Not willing to make the same mistake twice, Keaton saved his book to the computer and then the zip drive, sticking the latter in his pocket before shutting the computer down and making his way toward the stairs.

He stopped after making it to the second step, trying to make out the noise that had caught his attention the first time. The mumbling of a woman's voice caught his attention and he realized the entire event was indeed happening again! Keaton took two steps at a time, his calves and quads aching with every step to the point he wasn't sure if he could take another one.

His body had been ravaged from dehydration and hunger and now he was pushing it to his last breath. He stopped momentarily on the landing in order to catch his own breath and allow the cramps in his body to subside. However, the screams that were coming from the parents' room above him sent him into a frenzy and in no time he was standing in the middle of the hallway.

Even though the screams and cries had already died out, there was an obvious and pungent smell of blood and perspiration filling the entire second floor. The house was much too quiet for Keaton's liking and his hand trembled as he reached to turn on the hallway light. After the first couple of flips, there was no response.

There was a slight flicker from the light in the hall but there was not enough of an illumination for Keaton to see the entire hallway. He was almost positive he saw someone standing at the doorway of the master bedroom but there was no way of knowing for sure. Keaton wanted to walk toward the room but his body wouldn't physically allow him. Instead, his feet merely shuffled under him.

First the right one, then the left. Then the light above him flickered again, giving him a little better look at the hallway that spread out before him. Now, he was certain there was someone standing in the hallway. Keaton swore no matter who was in the bedroom, he would not allow them into the room with the kids again.

After shuffling a little further toward the entryway to the room, Keaton could feel someone moving toward him. In a panic, he took two steps backwards before being able to catch his breath enough to stop.

That's when the light bulb flickered one more time, this time better than all the other times. There he was as clear as day, standing in the hallway before Keaton. Taking in a deep breath, Keaton could feel the cold air invading each and every centimeter of his lungs as the being in front of him starting moving toward him.

"Stop right there!" Keaton screamed out at the unknown person in front of him. "You're not getting passed me tonight," he exclaimed, the words slipping from his lips before he had time to think them through.

In an instant, the lightbulb started strobing, only giving Keaton a glance at the being every few seconds before the light would go out. Every time it came on the person dressed in the long, hooded robe would be a step closer.

Before long, he was in an all-out sprint toward Keaton. The footsteps were heavy and determined and they gained on Keaton so quickly there was nowhere to go or turn to. Keaton closed his eyes but stood tall and didn't budge an inch. His would-be attacker stopped on a dime when he realized Keaton wasn't going to move.

Keaton waited on the impact, but there was none. Just a sickening laughter echoing down the hall past him. Shocked and disgusted, Keaton turned on his heels and looked toward the girls' room.

There he was. The mystery man robed in all black was standing at their doorway laughing hysterically at Keaton. He didn't know how he had gotten by him with him blocking the entire hallway but what mattered is that he had and now he was on his way to slaughter the little girls like he had done night after night for the past hundred or more years. The mocking laughter of the murderer boomed down the hallway toward Keaton and seemed to embrace him. The longer he listened to it the louder it seemed to get until he was sent into a blind fury he had only experienced a couple of times in his life.

Keaton raced toward the robed maniac who was now standing over the young girls. They were cowering and crying, trying to avoid his view by huddling together. Even though his laughter continued, their cries for help finally overwhelmed its horrific sound.

"You stupid son of a bitch."

Keaton didn't yell the words. Instead, he allowed them to slide off the end of his tongue with every morsel of hate he had for the person standing before him. The axe was raised high above the heads of the pre-teen girls but it slowly dropped to his side as he turned to face the man who just couldn't seem to take a hint. With a glimmer of hope on their face, the young girls cried out to the stranger for help, pleading, hoping, nearly praying, he was there to rescue them from the plight that had followed them day after day. Keaton had already decided he was willing to sacrifice himself and at this very moment he knew it may come to that.

The Axeman looked at Keaton with shock and dismay. Keaton had so many things played out in his mind to say if this opportunity ever rolled around but now, standing in front of the being that appeared to be seven feet tall, all words escaped him. He could feel the saliva in his mouth literally dissolving as he stood before the cloaked figure, mouth slightly ajar. Using just the tips of his middle fingers, Keaton wiped away some of the sweat that had collected there, binding his heated skin like glue. The Axeman shifted his head to the side to get a good look at the minion who was interrupting his nightly activity. It was clear he was unamused. Keaton watched the man carefully as he rotated the axe handle wildly with his right hand, the blade pointed toward Keaton on each half rotation as if he were going to throw it at him any moment. Keaton couldn't stand the pressure of the situation any longer. He had stopped the massacre of the children and now he had to get as far away as possible. Just as he started backing out of the room, Keaton saw the Axeman tilt his head back as his mouth flew open and that same sadistic laughter flowed from him like lava across Keaton's skin.

The laughter once again billowed through the house as the robed figured started toward Keaton bound and determined to get rid of the pest he was once and for all. The hallway was stifled with a darkness Keaton only witnessed a couple of times in his life but he fought through it to find the staircase. His eyes widened to adjust to the pitch black while his elongated fingers searched for the walls to guide his path.

Using nothing but his fingertips, Keaton moved through the hall as quickly as he could until he located the stairs leading down, deeper into the darkness that was the first floor. He could hear the laughter and heavy breathing gaining on him with every tiny step he took. He wildly searched for freedom behind every shadowed footstep. Finally Keaton was able to find the staircase and even though he couldn't see what was below the one he was on, he had no choice than to stride faithfully into the darkness. Thankfully his timing was perfect step after step and with each one, he was a little closer to escaping the killer who was closing in.

Keaton could hear the axe being dragged behind the man on his heels, splintering the oak floor with each of his footfalls.

"Don't run from me, boy," a voice crept out of the man gaining ground on him.

The voice was deep but broken. Chills started at Keaton's feet and worked their way to his chest and arms. He tried to shake them off but that was impossible. The shadow behind him was growing darker and taller with every step he took and Keaton knew there was no escaping him no matter how fast he ran.

"It's time for you to know exactly who you are Keaton," yelled out the being behind him. Keaton's name being called struck a cord and instantly made him wonder what he was talking about.

"Just keep moving," Keaton kept whispering to himself as he worked his way down the stairs toward the bottom floor, "you're almost there."

He was almost certain the robed figure was a demon and he knew from growing up in the Bible belt of south Mississippi that demons could take on any quality or characteristic they wanted in order to get exactly what they desired. Hell, he had experienced it first hand with his encounter with Rebecca, or whatever she was.

Keaton made it to the bottom step and leapt toward the door. He looked over his shoulder briefly to see how close the Axeman was. He was too close. Keaton was able to get the deadbolt unlocked before he was on top of him. By then the sweat on his hands and his trembling fingers made it impossible to turn the tiny lock at the bottom. Time after time he was sure he had a grip on it only to have it slip at the last second, with fresh air and a chance at freedom just a foot away. When the shadow had completely overwhelmed the doorway where Keaton was standing, he realized there was no chance at escaping. For the first time in all these days, Keaton was about to come face to face with the savage killer that had not only wreaked havoc on the Crescent City for all those years, but had also tormented the spirits of this family repeatedly for more than 100 years.

After taking a deep breath and swallowing the vomit that had already collected in his non drawn-up mouth, Keaton turned away from the door and into what was sure to be a fight for his life. The Axeman was just as big as he had appeared in the bedroom upstairs but Keaton refused to back down. Taking a deep breath and stepping forward, he was sickened to see a smile decorating the murderer's lips. The hood was darker than the night that had encompassed the home, covering the Axeman's entire face except for his dried, cracking lips. Looking as if they had been exposed to extreme temperatures of cold, the top layer of the skin on his lips hung loosely, in chunks. His yellowing, rotting teeth would grab piece after piece and pull it off in strips, in what seemed to be a nervous habit.

Keaton tried to keep himself calm but the stench the Axeman was putting off smells like the closest thing he had ever smelled to death. The smell wasn't just of a death that had been exposed to the elements for a couple of days. No, it was one that had been infested for years by maggots, worms, and the putrid waters of Orleans Parish.

"What do you want from me?" Keaton screamed into the monster's face before him, bowing his shoulders up slightly at the same time, hoping to make himself appear bigger than he actually was.

"I want the same thing we've had since you served as the Bavarian Ripper from 1806 to 1808 and took 50 to their grave. Or, remember the time in New South Wales between 1835 and 1841 when you took another ten down before you were hung in 1842? Undoubtedly you haven't forgotten all the fun you had through the centuries serving as a manipulator, servant, and messenger for the Angel of Death? You sure weren't regretful when you filled the role of the servant girl annihilator in Austin, Texas for an entire year, 1884 to 1885. I, to this day, don't know why you even stopped at eight victims," the Axeman stopped his badgering of Keaton momentarily to allow a hair-raising laugh to escape his wilted lips. "Am I ringing any bells with you Mr. Fordyce? I mean, this is the first life you've lived that you haven't taken a life. But that doesn't mean you haven't thought about it. Oh you've thought about it thousands of times, haven't you? Remember the time you planned how you could kill and dispose of Rebecca in the middle of the night and disappear with Caroline?"

Each word the Axeman spoke hit Keaton a little deeper, made him bleed a little more freely. He didn't remember anything the monster of a former man in front of him was telling him but he wanted to understand where all these details were coming from. He was terrified to know the truth but desperate to understand it at the same time.

"Only life? What the hell is that supposed to mean? I've only lived one life! I have only ever been Keaton Fordyce! None of these monsters you've brought up! You sir are a piece of shit!"

Keaton blasted back at him, hoping to strike the same nerves he had just been dealt. However, there was no such reaction on the face of the Axeman.

"Well, even if you don't remember some of your first mission, maybe you'll recall your most famous and profitable life of all. You sir were responsible for 68 murders from 1911 to 1919, some of them right here in New Orleans. You have been feared by millions and have even taken on the role of the proverbial boogie man to kids everywhere. You've had so much fun through the years in your different roles but I'm guessing from your facial expression you don't remember any of them either?"

Keaton was tired of hearing all this nonsense about him being some murderer in past lives and all the hell he put people through. He had simply had enough and he had to find a way to make him stop. Before he thought it through he lunged at the giant in front of him and landed a strong right against his left jaw. Keaton was certain he had been electrified as volt after volt of galvanizing power rushed through his veins, knocking him against the front door. He looked up from his new seat against the door and was even more pissed off to see the Axeman smiling back at him.

"Maybe this will make you believe," the hooded figure remarked as he placed both hands on his hood and pulled it back, revealing his entire face for the first time to Keaton.

"Oh my God," were the only words Keaton could manage to utter as he was now staring at his own face smiling back at him.

Chapter Twelve

KEATON WAS TRANSPORTED to a time he didn't recognize but yet he knew exactly where he was and what he was there to do. It was May 22, 1918 and Keaton, known as Joseph Delacroix then, was standing at the corner of Upperline and Magnolia. Even though the Mangion's wouldn't be his first victims they would come to symbolize the beginning of the Axeman's reign in New Orleans. The neighborhood was a quiet one, not affluent, and definitely unassuming. There was no way the Italian grocer and his wife could have known that hell was standing just a few feet away, out under the dim street light. It was two o'clock in the morning on a Wednesday, in a highly populated, working-class area. The houses, separated by just a few feet, were completely dark, their residents totally unaware that a murderer was in their midst.

Making his way slowly into the darkness, Keaton was aware of every step he was taking, even though he also knew he was actually in a mansion in New Orleans. He couldn't explain this any other way than it being a past life regression of sorts. He watched his steps closely, so as not to make any noise, but strangely it was like his feet already knew where they were going. The dew had collected on the early summer lawn and stifled any opportunity of noise to escape from the brand new Nettleton leather shoes that adorned his feet. Keaton remembered shelling out $10 for this new pair at the Maison Blanche on Canal Street. He couldn't believe he was now trekking them through the dew of an Upperline neighborhood. As he reached the backdoor of the simple two bedroom home he also realized that killing the occupants would surely get blood on them as well.

"Shit," he exclaimed angrily in a whisper, wishing he had had more of an opportunity to think this entire thing through before moving forward.

He looked the house over from that angle carefully and under an educated eye. He was not new at this so he had a reputation and a freedom to keep in check.

"No insulation. Very quiet house," he remarked as he held his right ear to the wall, a mere six feet from the neighbor's outer wall to their bedroom.

Just from there he could here old man Maggio snoring.

"I've got to be very, very quiet," Keaton thought, stepping off the back steps long enough to look for a tool for entry into the home.

He didn't have to look far. There was a wood chisel for breaking in and an axe for doing the dirty work. Keaton made it a point to never bring his own weapons to the scene of the crime. So far, he hadn't had to. Everybody in the south, and particularly in New Orleans, had an axe close by. By not bringing his own Keaton eliminated any opportunities the authorities might have at connecting a previous purchase of a tool to him.

"Why give them a reason to even look at you if the victims are going to supply their own murder weapon?" Keaton would say to himself sometimes. This mentality would often require him to do more research on a home or family before committing the crime.

However, in the long run, a little extra time spent on research and not in a cell in the Orleans Parish Jail, or even worse, Angola Prison, was worth it to him. Angola was the newer state prison near the Mississippi State line. Stories from some that did hard time there said it was basically the Alcatraz of the South. Any convict outside the gates would be shot instantly. No questions asked. Joseph had no desire to be put away in such an establishment.

Keaton squatted down on the steps next to the back door and got to work on chiseling a panel out of the wooden door. Using nothing but the chisel and a screwdriver, he had the panel popped out within a matter of minutes. A nervous hand reached into the house and unlatched the backdoor. The hardest part of his job was now done.

No matter how many times he did this and how many times he got away with it he was still terrified until the moment he walked away unscathed. Picking up his weapon of choice, Keaston eased the door open carefully and as quietly as he could, hoping the man of the house had not forgotten to oil the squeaky hinge.

He was in luck.

Once in the home, it wasn't hard to locate the bedroom where the sleeping couple lay. The man's snores could have easily been heard over the next three houses if anyone was actually listening.

Thankfully, the neighbors were probably used to snoring and weren't going to pay any attention to the noises coming from the home tonight either. As Keaton walked in he was pleasantly surprised to see a long handled razor blade with a couple of nicks in it sitting on the kitchen counter. Folding it up for possible use later, Keaton deposited it in his pocket.

Step by deliberate step, Keaton made his way toward the bedroom. None of his steps were heavy. He tested the planked wooden floor with each small step, waiting for a weak spot to cry out.

Finally, he stepped into the bedroom and assessed the situation quickly before he could be noticed by the slumbering couple. That's when he realized the razor would come in very handy in this particular murder. Considering the husband was in such a deep sleep, he needed to take the wife out of the equation first and then deal with the large Italian next to her.

Laying the axe down on the floor and taking the razor out of his pocket and flattening it, Keaton went straight toward the wife and in one swift movement had grabbed the back of her head with his left hand. He jerked it backwards toward the bed, and quickly ran the open blade as deeply as he could across her taut neck. His goal was simple. He not only wanted to kill her but he needed it to happen instantly. No hassle, fighting, or gargling. Just instantaneous death. He got his wish as Mrs. Cat Maggino's head was now barely attached to her shoulders, a direct indication of just how angry Keaton became during these attacks.

Now with his job half done he turned his attention to Joseph who was still sleeping soundly, completely unaware that his wife's own warm blood was now splattered all over him and pooling under her lifeless body.

Keaton returned the bloodied blade to his pocket and retrieved the axe. Promptly, he laid two hammering blows to the sleeping man, instantly drawing moans of pain and desperation. When it was clear that Mr. Maggino would no longer pose a threat to him, Keaton pulled some of his clothes out of the closet and changed in the bathroom, brazenly leaving his own bloodied and stained clothes in the sink.

The porcelain claw foot tub in the corner of the bathroom caught the axe and the blood that hadn't dripped in the bedroom instantly collected in the bottom of the stark white tub. Keaton didn't bother to rinse it off; there was no point.

Keaton finished buttoning up the denim shirt, turned off the bathroom light, and quietly left the house at Upperline and Magnolia. Locking the damaged backdoor as he left, Keaton disappeared into the thick New Orleans night.

Keaton suddenly found himself walking through another residential area. He knew it was later in the summer and even though he didn't know where he was, once again, he knew exactly where his targets were and what his job was. He had gotten a late start on this one and even though he knew the sun wouldn't be up until at least 7:00 am, he wished he had given himself a little more time to work with.

It was June 28, 1918, a little over a month since Keaton found himself in the Maggino residence. The method for this attack was no different than the first time, New Orleans started panicking. Keaton, hoping to throw off the authorities by slightly changing

MOs, was smart enough to bring his own chiseling tools this time. Like a pro, Keaton was standing inside Louis Beamer's neighborhood grocery at the corner of Dorgenois and LaHarpe Streets within just a few minutes. Keaton had found an axe and a hatchet in the backyard of the property on the woodpile.

"These idiots make my job way too easy," he stated as he pulled both blades out of chunks of dried oak that hadn't been split since the winter.

Most winters this far south weren't that bad but this particular winter the Crescent City had experienced everything from 80 degree temperatures and tornadoes to 17 degree temperatures with sleet and measureable snowfall. Most of the older generation swore the end of the world was just right around the corner and most probably wouldn't live to see the next winter. How else could they explain it?

Armed with two blades, Keaton walked into the bedroom where he assumed the couple were sleeping. As soon as he stepped into the room, he knew he made a terrible mistake.

"Who are you?" yelled Mr. Beamer from the bed, his voice startling the woman who was sleeping next to him.

Keaton, not ever wearing a mask and knowing in that instant he could be identified and exposed in the right light, did the only thing he knew to do, attack! Allowing the long handled axe to fall to the floor, Keaton took the hatchet out of his back pocket and gave Louis Bessemer a swift blow to the right temple. Keaton could feel the skull crunch and collapse below the impact of the blade like an eggshell crumbling in his hand. The first victim fell unconscious at his feet and he turned his sights on the now frantic female screaming and holding her hands in front of her face while sitting up in bed.

To say Keaton was emotionless would have been an absolute understatement. He calmly replaced the hatchet with the axe and promptly struck her just above her left ear; her screams falling silent instantly. Disgusted with how this mission had gone, Keaton quickly hung the axe up in the bathroom on a towel rack before slipping out of the house just a little before 5:30 am. He was just as pissed at himself as he was at the man for being awake. He had to get serious if he was going to carry out these next few assignments without getting caught.

He disappeared into the early morning darkness on Dorgenois Street, blending in quietly and easily with all the mill and dock workers headed out to make an honest day's wage, and waited patiently for the crimes to be discovered. Two days later, the Times-Picayune newspaper reported the accounts of both victims, who apparently lived. Keaton was stunned to say the least. Those were massive injuries he inflicted and he left them for dead. He had royally screwed this one up and he was going to be very lucky not to be caught or killed because of it. He would wait awhile before trying again, until August 5th, that was.

Chapter Thirteen

KEATON LEARNED LATER that even though he had foiled his last assassination attempt of Beamer and his woman companion, the results weren't all lost. The New Orleans Police had yet to start making a connection between the attacks. This meant Keaton's modus operandi had not yet been figured out even though he used the same one every single time. He couldn't laugh at their lack of being able to connect the dots but he hoped their inability to do their job would continue for a few more months.

Keaton picked up a paper for a quick read before heading out for his next stop and had his spirits lifted. He read that Charlotte Lowe, the mistress of Mr. Beamer, not only died in surgery the previous day but right before passing, had also accused Mr. Beamer as being her attacker.

"Could this be any easier?" Keaton asked himself as he dressed and prepared himself for his stop on Elmira Street. His modus operandi didn't change. It didn't have to. Breaking into these shotgun homes became quicker and easier each time he was petitioned to do so. Keaton wanted to try to commit these crimes at different times during the day and night in order to get the best out of the element of surprise. This particular evening he was shocked to find the residence on Elmira Street quiet, even though it was just a little after night fall. After a brief walk around the home, Keaton wasn't able to hear any voices and only assumed the occupants would be sleeping.

Located just a couple of blocks off the Mississippi River, Keaton instantly noticed most of the homes still had lights on and chatter could be heard seeping through the thin walls of the tiny homes. He had to make entry quickly and quietly and he did just that. After standing nervously in the entryway of the home for what seemed like ages, Keaton finally heard deep breathing coming from one of the two bedrooms at the back of the house.

He had brought his own short handled axe to the scene this time because he didn't want any surprises. Holding it close to his side, Keaton entered the bedroom and was instantly shocked and surprised to see only a female occupying the bed in front of him. Under the comforter was an obvious baby bump, protruding freely and displacing the covers slightly.

Keaton should have turned on his heels and left the house immediately. He had no business standing over this woman who was obviously 8 months or more pregnant. But the emotions he thought and had hoped would raid his body in that instant weren't there. The only thing that crossed his mind was he hated to mess up this pretty girl's face with his axe.

"Get the job done," a voice in his head called out to him in a frustrated tone. "You've been gazing at this whore for far too long."

Keaton seemed to snap out of his trace. He shook his head back and forth and blinked his eyes wildly until he was able to focus on the task at hand.

"He's probably right. She probably is a whore. If she wasn't, her husband would be here with her right?"

Keaton didn't mean a word of what he was thinking, he was just secretly hoping to shut the voices up that seemed to overwhelm his mind these days. That's when Mrs. Schilling awoke startled, finding a strange man lurking over her bed.

"Who are..?"

She wasn't able to get the final word out of her mouth before he promptly brought the blade down on her head, instantly knocking her unconscious. However, Keaton knew he didn't strike her as hard as he could and should have. At the last second, his damn emotions had gotten the best of him and he pulled off his power in the swing ever so slightly. Regardless, the blade found its mark and did become buried about two inches into the pregnant women's skull. Keaton stood and stared at his handy work a few more seconds before leaving the house, propping the bloody axe against the house as he left.

Keaton didn't wait around to see if anyone else was in the second bedroom. He wanted out and as far from this house as possible.

He couldn't wait to see what the newspaper reported the next morning and he didn't have to wait long to find out. According to the article, after the husband came home and found his wife, a man passing by the house found the axe and picked it up. A neighborhood police officer saw this and immediately tried to stop him, wondering if he had any part in the attack. He was arrested after running but was later found to not be involved. Mrs. Schilling did survive and also gave birth to a healthy baby girl a short time later. Keaton was stunned to feel relief take over his body when he read those words, but his emotions didn't stop there. The following day, he had fresh flowers delivered to Mrs. Schilling's room. The card wasn't signed to or from anyone.

By now Keaton had gotten the hang of his tasks and even though he had been frustrated with the failure of his previous attack, he didn't feel bad she was still alive. However, he couldn't leave any more victims alive from this point forward.

Five days later he had another target on his radar, Joey Palmeno. This was when Keaton finally earned his nickname, the Axeman. Gaining access to the home again by chiseling out a panel in the wooden door, Keaton realized there where occupants in both bedrooms. In the bedroom at the front of the house two women, and the bedroom behind that one, an older man. Making it a habit to always take out the strongest threat first, Keaton eased into the man's room, pulling his trademark short-handled axe from under his coat.

After a couple of swings on the man, Keaton realized this task was not going to be an easy one at all. The thuds of the blade against his skull and upper body seemed magnified at 3:00 am and Keaton knew he had to finish the job before waking the women in the other room. One final whack from the weapon seemed to do the job, but at this point Keaton could hear rustling in the room next door. Satisfied with the condition of the man in bed, he realized it was time to silence the girls in the other room.

He was stunned to see both sitting upright in bed when he came out of the bedroom.

"Uncle Joe?" a young female's voice called out, but when he didn't respond one of the girls let out a bloodcurdling scream that sounded as if it had awakened the entire neighborhood.

Keaton did the only thing he could think to do at that moment and it was to get the hell out of there. Even though the house was small the hallway guiding his exit seemed to roll on forever. The screams kept coming and he knew with each one, another neighbor was turning on their bedside lamp, wondering what all the commotion was. Finally Keaton was at the end of the hallway and out of the house. Within seconds, he had disappeared into the New Orleans darkness.

Finally making it back to his flat, Keaton quickly changed before settling in for a few hours of sleep. He would wait patiently for the newspaper to release information about the attack and the police's theories. If they were no closer than last time he could continue, but if they were finally catching on, and Keaton secretly hoped this cat and mouse game would get more interesting, then he would take a little time off and let the hysteria in town really start boiling before he attacked again.

The wait ended up being a short one. Just two days later the newspaper's headline screamed, "Is an Axeman at large in New Orleans?" Keaton was ecstatic. The people of New Orleans now knew he existed, were terrified, and the police weren't quite sure what to do to stop it. Never having been much of a fan of the police officers in the area, Keaton was a little stunned to read about one that felt like these weren't the Axeman's first kills.

John Dantonio was his name and after years as a detective he finally retired. However, he seemed to remember in 1911 there were four murders that fit this particular mold and now that they had started back, he wanted to share the information he had about it.

"Bravo detective! You sir would be right! Those were also mine!" Keaton dramatically stated to the black and white words in front of him, as if performing from a stage.

With New Orleans in an uproar, there was no doubt time would be taken off, but he would have to wait to see just how much time. For the next 6 months the folks of New Orleans went absolutely nuts. There were dozens of cases in which people claimed to have found a chisel at their backdoor or an axe lying on the ground, but none of these items were there because of Keaton. One man even heard someone at his backdoor and shot at the suspected intruder, but of course there was no one there.

Keaton enjoyed reading all these stories knowing he had a few crazies out there that were trying to copy his ways. He wasn't bothered by this and even thought it added more credibility to his own actions when he started back up. A city in the United States had never been so paralyzed in fear due to the actions of one person. But, truth be told, he was just getting started.

Exactly six months to the date of the last attack, the Axeman felt it was time to strike again. Even though New Orleans was already on edge because of the attacks, the next one was about to push them over the edge! On March 10, 1919 the small, immigrant community of Gretna was the target of the Axeman and the unfortunate victims were the Cassard family. The quaint, yet traditional New Orleans style home sat at the corner of Jefferson and Second Street.

Screams emitted from the home in the early morning hours drew neighbors to the young family's home. They were more than stunned at what they found when they entered the back bedroom. Mrs. Rosie Cassard's testimony was that she awoke to find a large man standing over her bed with an axe. She tried to protect her two-year old daughter Marilyn but one swing from the Axeman's blade caught the young child in the back of the head. After her husband Cavaille tried to fight off their attacker, he was also struck numerous times and mortally wounded.

Keaton left the Cassard family home with more emotion than he had ever felt before. He knew feeling such remorse could cost him his job and his life but he was disgusted by what he had just done. The people of New Orleans and Orleans Parish were equally as shocked by the horrific crime. After returning to his apartment, Keaton waited patiently for his next instructions. He wanted out. He just didn't want to do this anymore. Wishing such a thing would get him out of this pact quicker than he had ever intended but he was alright with that now. For the time being he still had orders to complete and he would do those to the best of his ability until his time as the Axeman was over.

Chapter Fourteen

JUST THREE DAYS AFTER the horrendous attack on the Cassard Family, the Axeman sent a letter to the editor of the Times-Picayune newspaper. It shook the residents of Crescent City and nearly brought the city to its knees. Most of the residents had their own ideas of who the Axeman was and many thought he was the Devil himself. Many that thought the latter had their worst fears validated a little more. The letter soon found its way into every newspaper in the New Orleans area and read as follows:

Esteemed Mortal:

They have never caught me and they never will. They have never seen me, for I am invisible, as the ether that surrounds your earth. I am not a human being, but a spirit and a fallen demon from the hottest hell. I am what you Orleanians and your foolish police call the Axeman.

When I see fit I shall come again and claim other victims. I alone know who they shall be. I shall leave no clue except my bloody axe, besmeared with the blood and brains of him whom I have sent below to keep me company.

If you wish you may tell the police not to rile me. Of course I am a reasonable spirit. I take no offense at the way they have conducted their investigation in the past. In fact, they have been so utterly stupid as to amuse not only me but His Satanic Majesty, Francis Josef, etc. But tell them to beware. Let them not try to discover what I am, for it were better that they were never born than to incur the wrath of the Axeman. I don't think there is any need of such a warning, for I feel sure the police will always dodge me, as they have in the past. They are wise and know how to keep away from all harm.

Undoubtedly, you Orleanians think of me as a most horrible murderer, which I am, but I could be much worse if I wanted to. If I wished, I could pay a visit to your city every night. At will I could slay thousands of your best citizens, for I am in close relationship to the Angel of Death.

Now, to be exact, at 12:15 (earthly time) on next Tuesday night, I am going to visit New Orleans again. In my infinite mercy, I am going to make a proposition to you people. Here it is:

I am very fond of jazz music, and I swear by all the devils in the nether regions that every person shall be spared in whose home a jazz band is in full swing at the time I have mentioned. If everyone has a jazz band going, well then, so much the better for you people. One thing is certain and that is that some of those people who do not jazz it on Tuesday night (if there be any) will get the axe.

Well, as I am cold and crave the warmth of my native Tartarus, and as it is about time I leave your earthly home, I will cease my discourse. Hoping that thou wilt publish this, and that it may go well with thee, I have been, am, and will be the worst spirit that ever existed either in fact or realm of fantasy.

The Axeman

That night, New Orleans partied like it was Fat Tuesday! Every bar, club, and house in the entire city blared jazz music and the Axeman must have been pleased because the city was quiet and its residents rested comfortably for a couple of months until August 10, 1919, 5 months since his last attack. That particular night a sleeping grocer was attacked but survived and police found the bloodied axe propped against the counters in the kitchen.

A week later on September 3, 1919, the Axeman chose a different method of entry purely by accident, possibly confusing the authorities. Keaton had forgotten his chisel so he had to break in through a bedroom window. Nineteen year old Sara Allary was struck numerous times while sleeping in her bed on Second Street but somehow survived her gruesome injuries.

Finally, on October 27, 1919, the Axeman would claim his last victim in New Orleans. The door at the Baligant home was chiseled out a little after midnight that night and Mike Baligant was viciously attacked. Blood was splattered all over the walls and even covered the painting of Virgin Mary that was directly above Mr. Baligant's bed.

Keaton was instantly thrown back into the house in the Garden District of New Orleans and was obviously shaken and weak from all he had just learned.

Chapter Fifteen

"**D**OES ANY OF THIS RING a bell to you yet?" asked the monster of a man standing in front of him.

"Yes," he whispered his response as he remembered every single one of those attacks and everything he did to each of those people. "I was the Axeman."

He couldn't believe the words that had just escaped his lips but they were the truth no matter how you looked at it.

"Here's one more thing I bet you don't remember," the embodied Axeman stated as he threw Keaton back in time once more.

Keaton looked around nervously trying to make sense of where he was and why he was there. That's when he saw her. It was Mrs. Baligant, the wife of his last victim! He knew in that instant why he was here. She calmly raised her gun and fired one shot into Keaton, or Joseph Delacroix's chest, killing him instantly.

On that fateful night when he had broken in to their home and murdered Mr. Baligant, she had fallen asleep on the couch earlier in the evening and hid under the kitchen table as she heard her husband being murdered. Thinking there was no one else in the home, Keaton had taken his time. Taking his mask off, making himself a sandwich with their fresh deli meat, and even listening to a little bit of the radio. Mrs. Baligant sat quietly for hours until Keaton left her home. She reported what she witnessed to police but there was never enough evidence to get him arrested. Plus, she was a grieving widow who had witnessed her husband being murdered. How clear would her memory be anyway? After selling the family business, she sought out to stalk and murder Keaton at the first chance she got. She had tracked his killing spree to Baton Rouge, Lafayette, Beaumont, San Antonio, El Paso, Tucson, and now, Long Beach, California. Keaton had just finished dinner at Breakers when she stepped out from around the corner of the building and fired one shot from her Roth-Sauer pistol, striking him once in the chest.

She waited around for the police to show up and told them that this was the Axeman of New Orleans and the man that had killed her husband over a year ago and more than 2,000 miles away.

Keaton gasped for air as if he had been shot again. His right hand instantly went to his chest and the birthmark that looked identical to a bullet hole.

"All makes sense now doesn't it?" the past version of himself asked as Keaton collapsed against the front door.

Chapter Sixteen

A S PROMISED, on the morning of the tenth and final day, Ross was there for Keaton. He had played in his mind over and over again what he might find when he returned to the home and mentally prepared himself for the worst possible scenario. Ross knew Keaton was weak when he went in, but take away the one vice that gave him any strength or understanding, and it may be just enough to make him crack.

The sun had risen brilliantly over the Garden District that morning and even though spring was a couple of weeks ago, there was still in a chill in the air. More so in the car with Ross, where he sat, staring at the house for several minutes before opening the door. Even though everything appeared okay from the outside, he knew there very well may be a different story on the inside.

Chill bumps ravaged his body from his feet to the top of his head and nausea crept into his throat as he exited his car. Holding the open car door with his right hand, Ross leaned toward the curve as far as he could and gagged. Nothing came rushing from his body like he was sure was about to happen. He knew the nerves of whatever called this place home, coupled with the condition he may find Keaton in had simply gotten the best of him. But there was no way to avoid it. If his best friend was in trouble, it was time to go get him.

Now with a mission on his mind, Ross closed his car door and headed toward the gate. Even though his hands indicated their nervousness, the gate opened with ease. By the time it slammed behind him, he was in a near sprint for the front door, the desperate feeling in the pit of his stomach growing with every second that passed.

He was horrified to see that the front door of the home was actually cracked open, but as he tried to push the door open a little he could tell it was stuck on something. That's when he saw Keaton Fordyce's lifeless body laying behind it. Underneath him was a manuscript, over 300 pages in length, documenting his experiences in the home.

"Keaton!"

Ross rolled Keaton on his back and was horrified by the weight his normally stout friend had lost just over the course of the last ten days.

"Keaton, I need you to look at me!" Ross slapped at Keaton's face in an effort to make him wake up.

There was still no response.

"Shit!" he yelled in frustration, as he leapt from his position on the floor and made his way to the kitchen, glancing around wildly for a cloth to wet.

Finally, there was one in the sink. Running it under cold water, Ross left the water running and let the rag drip tiny ringlets of water all over the floor all the way out to his fallen comrade. Ross flattened it out and placed it on Keaton's face, hoping it would be enough to bring him back around.

"Keaton, it's all over. I'm getting you out of here."

Even though Keaton was exhibiting some shallow breathing, there was still no response and his pupils were fixed. Ross rubbed his eyes in both fear and desperation and realized he needed to make a decision. Without wasting another minute he did just that.

Pulling his phone out of his jeans pocket he dialed the three numbers no one ever wants to call.

"Yes, I need an ambulance. My friend is unresponsive."

Chapter Seventeen

THE DAY ROSS FOUND KEATON unresponsive, he was very near death. Upon arriving at Ochsner Medical Center, Keaton was found to be in withdrawals after detoxing from alcohol for the past ten days. In addition, he was dehydrated, his electrolytes were completely out of whack, and he had a massive urinary tract infection. The best the doctors in the emergency room could figure was Keaton had become so completely overwhelmed by the effects of the detox that he stopped eating and drinking. When they asked him how long it had been since he had eaten he honestly couldn't remember. He specifically remembered eating on day 5 but everything after that was just a blur.

When Keaton was at his most critical Ross was able to track down Rebecca with the help of an Alabama Highway Patrol friend. He was sure she would tell him that whatever situation Keaton was in was his own damn fault. But, surprisingly, she rushed right over that afternoon, leaving Caroline with her grandparents.

Keaton remained in ICU on a ventilator for six days while his body worked on getting strong enough to breath on his own again. He slept for another day when the ventilator was removed.

Rebecca stayed by his side each time there were visiting hours, 10:00 am, 2:00 pm, and again at 6:00 pm. Each time only for an hour, but she didn't miss one visit. Even though they didn't speak a word for more than a week, Rebecca could tell there was something different about her ex-husband. Something felt normal again. Almost like the first day she had met him.

Keaton began panicking as soon as he saw Rebecca sitting in the chair next to his bed. He wasn't one hundred percent sure he was even alive at the moment, but he hoped this wasn't the demon from the house.

"Am I dead?" he asked, waiting for a response from the woman sitting beside him.

He honestly expected her to lunge at him at any given moment.

"No, Keaton. This is really happening. I'm here," Rebecca answered with the same soft voice he remembered years ago.

"What happened?" he asked more to himself than anyone in general as thousands of scenes flashed before his eyes.

"Ross found you unconscious behind the front door. He had to call an ambulance. What all do you remember?"

He knew that question would come up before long. He desperately wanted to blurt out everything he remembered but decided to withhold that information until a later date.

"A little bit but not much," he responded.

"Do you remember working on this?"

Rebecca sat a folder on his lap. He picked it up with both hands and squeezed the corners. He could feel the ridges of the unevenly stacked papers and realized he really had written while he was in that house, though he only actually remembered being at his computer two or three times the entire stay.

A smile crept across his face as he reached into the folder and held the 300 typed pages to his chest.

"Oh my God, I was so scared this was part of a terrible dream," he exclaimed, holding the manuscript so tightly it appeared he was trying to detect a heartbeat from the pages.

"Keaton, I read it."

Hearing those words exit her mouth immediately drew his attention. The way the words were spoken came with a hint of fear and apprehension. He stared at her blankly for what seemed like an eternity before she spoke.

"It's better than the first one. It's the best book I've ever read."

Keaton exhaled audibly.

"Another question he knew would eventually be asked, a question he really didn't know how to answer.

"Can I tell you something and you not think I'm crazy?" Keaton asked, regretting even bringing it up as soon as the words slipped off his tongue.

He still couldn't believe she was even here and now he was going to scare her away with this 'don't think I'm crazy shit.'

"Never mind!" he blurted out before Rebecca could answer.

"I'm not going to think you're crazy. You just had a traumatic experience detoxing alone and without medicine. That's enough to drive someone crazy but no, I'm not going to think you're crazy. Talk to me."

"I think I had help by something or someone in the house to write the book. I know that sounds ridiculous but I only actually remember writing for three days. There's no way in hell I was able to get 107,000 typed words on a brand new book in ten days. Ten days, Rebecca."

"What is in that house that could have helped you on this book?"

Her response was more careful and understanding than what he had expected.

"Becca, there's a lot of bad things still trapped in that house," he answered her question without taking his eyes off of her.

He had to see her full response to what he had just revealed. She listened intently but chose not to respond right away. Finally, she started to speak.

"Keaton, I'm not doubting you for one minute. But, there are the possibilities of visual and auditory hallucinations when you detox on your own and many times, when it goes wrong, you end up seizing. Then, it's hard to make out what was real and what was your imagination," Rebecca explained to her ex-husband as gently as she could in hopes not to agitate him.

"You're probably exactly right," he responded out of kindness rather than agreement.

He knew based on how quietly she was talking she was trying to make them both believe the words she was speaking. There was no need for him to ruin the opportunity at hand by defiantly disagreeing with her. He could continue to know his truth and she could remain in hers.

Over the next few days, Keaton started eating more, ingesting tons of fluids, and getting stronger than he was when he walked into the house. Because of how terrifying and life-changing the events in that house were, Keaton couldn't get them out of his head. He dared think it, but a part of him wanted to go back and stay again, minus the detox. He couldn't help but wonder how many of his experiences were brought on by his detox.

After eleven days in the hospital, Keaton was set to be released. He awoke early, dressed, ate breakfast, and started reading over his manuscript, making a few changes here and there with his red pen in hand. Parts of the book were pure genius. It reminded him so much of his first book and he knew after reading it all the way through he had a fantastic opportunity to be a best-selling author again.

Rebecca had been staying with him the entire time. He told her time and time again she was more than welcome to stay at the Brent House, the hotel attached to the hospital, but she refused. Keaton's heart had never pushed her completely out. The reason they left was out of fear for him. Still, he was desperately trying not to say or do anything that might scare her. He wasn't sure if she was here because he almost died or because she still felt something for him.

Keaton's stomach rolled and rumbled in anxiousness as he thought about how things were going to come to an end today. Two things could possibly happen and both made him nervous. Either he would be leaving for Natchez alone, without Rebecca, or they would be back in each other's lives, attempting to work it out. Even though she hadn't mentioned anything regarding the second option, she was there and that was enough for him to know she still loved him.

"Hey, brought you a snack from the coffee shop," Rebecca announced as she walked back into the room, interrupting his train of thought at just the right time.

She held the bag behind her back but Keaton could hear it rustling against her legs as she walked in.

"Oh, really?" he smiled as she made her way to the side of his bed.

"Ta-Da!" Rebecca exclaimed, pulling out a blueberry scone, a side of fresh fruit, and chocolate milk.

Keaton's excitement took his voice away as a smile spread across his face.

"My God, you know me so well," he exclaimed, looking at the spread in front of him that just put his hospital breakfast to shame.

Rebecca smiled, leaned down and kissed him.

The entire world went silent for what seemed like an eternity.

"I'm sorry. I don't know what came over me," Rebecca broke the silence, lowering her head and eyes to the floor.

"Don't apologize, please. You did nothing wrong. Truth be told, I would love for me and you to give us a chance again. I know I ruined everything we had in the past but I'm good and sober now. That's the only reason I decided to take Ross' deal, in hopes if I got sober, then we might have another chance."

Keaton blurted out all those words before he even had a chance to filter through them. Rebecca stared at him for a second before taking a deep breath.

"Keaton, when Ross called me and told me about your condition, I never hesitated in coming. I realized on the drive here even though we have not talked in two years, I still love you, and always will. I had hoped this day would come sooner than later. I say all of that to say, I would love for us to try again."

She leaned in and kissed him again, this time harder and more passionate than any he had ever remembered before.

Something was finally going Keaton's way.

Ross offered them the house until Keaton could get back on his feet and they decided exactly what they wanted to do.

It was true, they were going to be a family again.

Chapter Eighteen

THE NEXT SIX MONTHS was a blur for the Fordyce family. Keaton had completely finished his book, queried six publishing companies, and was able to choose whom he wanted to publish it. He ultimately decided on Tomilson Press out of New York City. $600,000 for signing a contract and $250,000 for the next three novels, wasn't a bad deal for a man who had earned less than $10,000 a year on book revenues for the last two years.

Ross allowed them to stay in the house, rent-free until they could get back on their feet. However, the family made an offer on the home and would be moving in as soon as they could gather Keaton's belongings in Natchez and Rebecca and Caroline's in Mobile.

They had lived in their new home a little over four months when Keaton's new book was released. Overnight, it shot to number one on the New York Times best seller's list and on Amazon. The next morning Keaton and Rebecca lay in bed, discussing their new life, new home, and the tour Keaton would be going on soon.

"I want you and Caroline to travel with me to all my signings and appearances, if possible," Keaton remarked, while Rebecca lay on his outstretched arm, her head nestled against his shoulder and chest.

Rebecca knew he was afraid of relapsing to the animal he had become during the previous tour. She didn't have to remind him, it seemed to always be on his mind.

"Any of them we can be at, I promise we will be," she replied, giving him just enough comfort that he exhaled deeply.

They both were silent for a few seconds, staring at the ceiling. The house was deathly quiet, something Keaton was not used to. Every few seconds they could hear a car passing in front of the house on 3rd Street but besides that, the home sounded as empty as a tomb.

"Do you hear Caroline?" Rebecca asked, sitting up in bed and turning her head slightly in order to hear better.

Keaton didn't hear her initially, but sat up next to his wife and listened carefully. In the stillness of the home, he could hear her small voice.

"Yeah, I wonder who she's talking to?" Keaton asked, afraid to know the answer.

Rebecca slowly got up from the bed, trying not to make any noise, and tip-toed to the door. Once open, they could hear Caroline clearly now.

"But are y'all going to share your room with me now?" they heard their young daughter asked.

"Caroline, come here for a second baby," Rebecca called out to her, needing to lay eyes on her only child.

"Hi, mommy!" the blond with a headful of curls came bouncing into the doorway of the bedroom.

"Hi, baby! Who are you talking to in your room?"

Keaton knew exactly who she was talking to.

"My new friends! They used to live here too! They lived in my room," she tried to explain as clear as she could to her mother.

Keaton's arms covered in chills when he realized that everything he had experienced in that house was indeed true, maybe just a little embellished due to his natural detox. But he remembered hearing and seeing those girls very clearly.

Rebecca glanced at Keaton with wild eyes.

"Well, tell your friends its time for breakfast, so you'll have to come back and play later," Rebecca explained, crawling out of bed to go prepare breakfast for her family.

Caroline rushed to the doorway of her bedroom, put her tiny hands on each side of the door and leaned in.

"I've got to go eat breakfast. I'll be back in a little bit!"

Just as Rebecca was standing even with her, a red plastic ball came bouncing out of the room and into the hall. Rebecca stared at it in shock as it reflected off the railing of the upstairs balcony.

Rebecca froze, moving her head slowly to get a look into the room where she knew nobody was present.

"Keaton," she whispered at first, not able to get the words out of her mouth. "Keaton!" she yelled when she had finally caught her breath.

Keaton ran to stand beside his wife, looking down at the little red ball that was now lying still against Rebecca's foot.

"That...that ball...came out of that room. Keaton, there's no one in there," she tried to explain to her husband, who knew all too well about the movement of this house.

Keaton knelt down at his wife's feet and picked up the ball and bounced it back into the room. It struck the closet door and scampered slowly towards the bed where it stopped. The couple's eye's never left the plastic ball that was now completely still in front of Caroline's bed.

"You can throw it back to us," Keaton mentioned to the young girls who had inhabited that room for far too long. "We aren't going to hurt you."

Rebecca slowly traced Keaton's entire face with her eyes before looking back at the ball. She didn't know what to think.

Within seconds, the ball begin bouncing toward the couple.

"What the hell did I just witness?" Rebecca whispered to Keaton.

Before he answered, he tossed the ball back into the room.

"Keaton, did we buy a haunted house?" Rebecca asked, with confusion and fear in her eyes.

"It's not as bad you think," he started. "Let's go downstairs and I'll explain everything."

Rebecca started breakfast while Keaton tried to figure out what he would and wouldn't tell her. He had to tell her about the murders that took place but he figured he would hold off on bringing up the cloaked figure. Just the minor, safe details for now.

He plopped down on the couch in the living room and within a few seconds, Rebecca joined him.

"Ok, I need you to tell me what you know," she commanded of him, turning to face him on the couch.

"Ok, but please listen to me all the way through, ok?" Keaton instructed Rebecca before continuing.

Rebecca nodded her head, agreeing to his command.

"When I moved in, there was weird stuff going on here. Kids laughing, toy balls rolling down the steps, knocks on the door, and even footsteps and voices. But, all of that was just startling. When I began detoxing, that's when the nasty skeletons in my closet and this house started coming out. But those were only here because of where I was mentally and emotionally. The ones present here now aren't here to hurt us. They're just residual. I faced off with one of the bad ones just before I blacked out and I haven't felt him here again," Keaton explained, telling Rebecca most of the story but not all of it.

"I wonder why they're just now starting up. We've been here almost 6 months off and on?" Rebecca asked, trying her hardest to take in everything that was suddenly going on.

Keaton didn't have an explanation for that, only he knew they were there. Maybe they were trying to get used to him and his family being there.

"Since we are talking about the house, can I ask you something?" Rebecca asked in a tone that made Keaton nervous.

It was the same tone of voice that mothers used when telling a child they've been caught doing something wrong.

"Sure, what's wrong?" he asked, thinking he couldn't have already screwed up this new relationship with her.

"I woke up this morning around 3:00 am and you weren't in bed. I got up and looked throughout the house and you weren't here, Keaton. I don't care if this is the Garden District, Mid-City, or the French Quarter, nothing good happens in New Orleans at 3 in the morning. Where were you?"

Keaton took a deep breath and grabbed his wife's hands.

"Since I've been clean I have a hard time sleeping every night. Most nights I get up and go into my office to read or write and other times I lay here and stare at the ceiling under daylight. But some nights, I just have to get out of the house and go walk. I usually walk down to 1st Street and work my way back to the house. I can usually fall right to sleep when I return. I've been doing this at least once a week since we moved in this house. I'm surprised you hadn't found out before now, to be honest."

Rebecca stared at him for a minute. Searching his face for anything that would make her think he was lying.

"Well, just tell me these things. I know you've been alone for a while and are having a hard time giving up the independence you've had but you can talk to me and tell me anything. We can't afford to keep secrets from each other."

"You're exactly right and when it happens again, I'll at least leave a note on my pillow or something."

"Thank you, baby," Rebecca said with a smile as she leaned in and kissed Keaton softly on the lips.

There was no need to tell her what he was really doing out at 3 in the morning.

Chapter Nineteen

KEATON FORDYCE SAT in the chair behind a table full of his new novel, "Delirium." The line stretched around The Rink and doubled back to the Garden District Book Shop where he sold more than 2,000 pre-ordered books and had another 3,000 stacked in boxes behind him. If you had told him a year ago he would have another book out, Keaton would have scoffed. There was no way that could have come true without his stay in the house. However, the posters adorning the windows and walls of the New Orleans bookstore proved that Keaton Fordyce had once again become a New York Times Best Seller. The line stretched from just outside of the book store to the next block. Many of those in line were former college and fraternity buddies whom Keaton had not seen in years. Others were former fans who thought they would never again see his name in print and still others who had never actually heard of him but supported the local bookstores whenever there was a signing. Keaton especially liked that last group of shoppers.

Sitting next to him, placing sticky notes on the covers of how the books should be signed, was his loving wife. He knew if he could ever prove himself to her again they could be the happy family they once were. Sitting behind her on the floor was now 5 year old Caroline, working diligently on her coloring book of Natchez. He finally had his life back and there was nothing that was ever going to take it away from him again.

New Orleans, what he now considered his hometown, was only the first stop on a 60 city tour scheduled for that winter and early spring. He was excited he and Rebecca could get back to their bucket list items, all while making money and spending time with their child. He was excited about this new life now ahead of him and he knew this was only the beginning of wonderful things ahead for the Fordyce Family.

Chapter Twenty

KEATON STEPPED OUT the front door of their Garden District home at 8:00 am and could already see steam rising from 3rd Street on this sultry November morning.

"Welcome to life in the South," Keaton mumbled to himself.

Just last week he had completed a signing in Chicago as snow blew in from Lake Michigan. Now, in the dead of winter in New Orleans, the humidity had already risen above 80% and the temperature wasn't far behind that.

"Ahh, what a beautiful day," he remarked to himself as he bounded down the hand full of steps and onto the walkway in front of the house. He wore nothing more than boxer shorts and flip flops. Making his way to the front gate he could see the Sunday edition of The Times-Picayune lying on the brick sidewalk.

"Hi Daddy!"

He heard the tiny but powerful voice calling from the second floor of the home. He looked up and found Caroline standing at the open window in her bedroom, peering out at him through the screen.

"Hi baby!" he called back to her.

He looked at the house from top to bottom, each curve, edge, window, single, and step. He smiled at the home. In all honesty, Keaton owed this house his life and would have never gotten sober, written another book, or had his family back if it weren't for the hell this house put him through.

He had come to grips with a lot of the events that had taken place in the house and could now easily blame them on his all natural detox. It may have almost killed him, but the results far outweighed the ten days he spent there.

Stepping outside the iron gate, Keaton glanced around to make sure none of his neighbors were seeing his attire. When he was sure the coast was clear, he slid the paper out of its protective plastic covering.

"Third murder in as many days. Has the Axeman returned to New Orleans?" screamed the headline as soon as Keaton opened the paper, in a font usually reserved for local natural disasters.

Keaton stumbled backwards slightly on the incline of the driveway. Sweat pooled around his brow and upper lip. He licked the salty substance from sharp hairs protruding from his unshaven face. A smile crept across his lips. He was proud of his work. He had been chosen and he wasn't going to stop until he was caught. Keaton knew the truth though. They didn't catch him before and they sure as hell wouldn't catch him this time around. Life after life, century after century, and victim after bloody victim, he would continue killing, his reason to live. As long as he was capable he would come as ether in the night and do the work he was destined to do.

Keaton, with his handsome yet rugged appearance, smiled and winked.

His secret is safe with you, right?

About the Author

BRANDI PERRY was born and raised in Columbia, Mississippi. Those closest to Brandi knew she was destined to be a writer from an early age.

She is an avid traveler and adventurer, and all of Brandi's novels include the places that are dear to heart. More time than not, you can see a little bit of her hometown in every book.

After graduating from the University of Southern Mississippi with degrees in English and History, Brandi sidelined her dream of becoming an attorney by entering the education field. She taught for six years before emergency brain surgery detoured her daily life. As part of the therapy process, Brandi started writing and within a year after her surgery, *Wayward Justice* was released. Her second novel, *A Whisper on the Bayou*, was nominated for the Mississippi Library Association Fiction Book of the Year. *Buried Cries* was released in 2012 and immediately brought home Publish America's Fiction Cover of the Year Award. That same year, Brandi was asked to represent the State of Mississippi during Arts and Literature Month, an honor she held from 2012-2015 and 2018. In 2014, with the release of *The Jury*, Brandi was nominated for the Mississippi Governor's Art Award and in 2017 she was Runner-Up for the Signature Magazine Author of the Year Award.

Brandi still resides in south Mississippi and in her free time she enjoys working her Backroads and Burgers food and travel blog, volunteering in Columbia, going to the beach, spending time with her friends and family, and watching a variety of sports.

Available from Shotwell Publishing

GOLD-BUG MYSTERIES (Mystery & Suspense Imprint)

Billy Jo by Michael Andrew Grissom

To Jekyll and Hide by Martin L. Wilson

Splintered: A New Orleans Tale by Brandi Perry

GREEN ALTAR BOOKS (Literary Imprint)

A New England Romance & Other SOUTHERN Stories by Randall Ivey

Tiller (Clay Bank County Series) by James Everett Kibler

NONFICTION TITLES

A Legion of Devils: Sherman in South Carolina by Karen Stokes

Annals of the Stupid Party: Republicans Before Trump (The Wilson Files) by Clyde N. Wilson

Carolina Love Letters by Karen Stokes

Confederaphobia: An American Epidemic by Paul C. Graham

The Devil's Town: Hot Springs During the Gangster Era by Philip Leigh

Dismantling the Republic by Jerry C. Brewer

Dixie Rising: Rules for Rebels by James R. Kennedy

Emancipation Hell: The Tragedy Wrought By Lincoln's Emancipation Proclamation by Kirkpatrick Sale

Lies My Teacher Told Me: The True History of the War for Southern Independence by Clyde N. Wilson

Maryland, My Maryland: The Cultural Cleansing of a Small Southern State by Joyce Bennett.

My Own Darling Wife: Letters from a Confederaate Volunteer. Edited with introduction by Andrew P. Calhoun

Nullification: Reclaiming Consent of the Governed (The Wilson Files) by Clyde N. Wilson

The Old South: 50 Essential Books (Sothern Reader's Guide) by Clyde N. Wilson

Punished with Poverty: The Suffering South by James R. & Walter D. Kennedy

Segregation: Federal Policy or Racism? by John Chodes

Southern Independence. Why War? by Dr. Charles T. Pace

Southerner, Take Your Stand! by John Vinson

Washington's KKK: The Union League During Southern Reconstruction by John Chodes.

When the Yankees Come: Former South Carolina Slaves Remember Sherman's Invasion. Edited with introduction by Paul C. Graham

The Yankee Problem: An American Dilemma (The Wlson Files) by Clyde N. Wilson